EVA LAURENSON
Amantos

About the Author

Eva Laurenson was born in Berlin, Germany. After studying agricultural sciences at the Humboldt University of Berlin, she studied and worked in the field of animal breeding and quantitative genetics in the Netherlands and Scotland. After earning a PhD, she moved to Australia in 2013, where she wrote and directed screenplays and short theatre plays while continuing to work as a scientist.

In 2022, she is planning to move back to her hometown of Berlin as a full-time writer.

www.evalaurenson.weebly.com

Eva Laurenson

AMANTOS

TO PARADISE AND BACK

Fantasy Novel

cub & calf

1. Edition
Approved Paperback-Edition March 2022
Copyright © 2022 cub & calf publishing,
129 Kirkwood Street,
Armidale, NSW, Australia
All rights reserved.
Cover and Layout by Eva Laurenson
Edited by Nicola Hodgson
Root and Branch Editing
www.root-and-branch-editing.com
ISBN 978-0-6453396-8-0

For all the star-crossed lovers

and

Yan

Chapter 1

Nepomuk woke up. His neck was stiff from lying on the hard and dusty ground, his eyes were uncomfortably dry and heavy, and the noises around him were unfamiliar. It sounded as if hundreds, maybe even thousands or millions, of feet sloshed, scraped, and scurried around him. Blurry at first, he squinted into a cloudless sky. He was not in his bed, and all around him millions of people became reality.

He sat up and gagged. A round and metallic-tasting object had slipped down his throat. Following a gut-wrenching heave, he pulled a large gold coin from his mouth. He looked around for the prankster who thought it funny to stick money down a sleeping man's throat; he could have choked and died. But the people around him looked just as confused as he felt. In fact, people around him didn't just look confused, some of them looked horrifically mangled. Most were just old like Nepomuk, but some had missing limbs, gaping wounds, or holes in places that were surely not healthy. And the children looked as though they might drop from consumption any minute. Had there been an attack, or an earthquake, maybe?

Nepomuk felt his head to see if he had been struck by something that would explain amnesia, then patted down his arms, his chest, and finally his legs as far as he could reach. Nothing seemed broken, and there was no blood. In truth, he felt no pain despite being somewhat stiff. He was wearing his favourite brown trousers, which were comfortably bulging around his knees, and a white shirt that he had been given last Christmas, if he remembered correctly. His physical integrity calmed him a little, but he was still confused as to where he was and how he had gotten here. Maybe this was all a dream. He was inspecting the coin in his hand, still upset that someone had stuck it down his throat, when someone close to him spoke.

"That should give you a fine fare," said an old, gangly man next to Nepomuk.

"What?"

"That obolus. Should give you a premium seat."

"What are you talking about? Who are you?" Nepomuk's anger rose as he didn't wake up from this nightmare and his confusion did not dissolve with this stranger's words.

"I'm sorry. I cannot tell you who I am," said the man.

"What, Secret Service?" scoffed Nepomuk.

"That sounds intriguing, but I don't think so," the man mused.

"Well, can you at least tell me where we are?"

"We are in Epipedo," said the man, who was dressed in some brown-and-green loden cloth that seemed at least fifty years out of fashion.

"Epipedo?"

"The plains. The plains before the River Styx."

The man must have lost his marbles. Nepomuk had heard of the River Styx. A long time ago, when he was in school, he had read *The Iliad*, learned about Odysseus and all the other Greek heroes who had crossed the river into the underworld on their lion-hearted adventures. None of these mythological stories ever mentioned Epipedo or millions of people waiting at the shores of the river. But then, with people dying all the time, there must always have been people waiting for their transport across the river, even when Odysseus had dropped by. Homer probably didn't think it necessary to mention them.

A foggy memory crept into Nepomuk's head.

"You remember," said the old man. "You must have been pretty out of it when it happened."

"When what happened?" Nepomuk was almost crying from frustration.

"Death."

"Death? You mean ... I'm not ... I'm not dead, this is just a dream!"

The old man just smiled at him.

"I'm not dead."

Panic strapped itself around his chest. Eyeballs hanging from their sockets stared at him, gaunt faces hovered in the masses of oncoming people, and the foggy memory wafted in his head, teasing him.

His son had sat beside him, his head bowed to his chest. His daughter had opened a window, and the sweet spring air had moved the curtains. His wife had murmured silent prayers, her dark brown eyes half closed and staring into an invisible void.

"What nonsense! Is this a prank? Like pupils who moved all their classroom furniture out into the yard? Someone put me here. Was it my son? He did that with the classroom furniture, you know."

"I don't think it was your son. At least I would hope not, because that would mean he's dead, like you."

"I'm not dead!" Nepomuk scrambled up as quickly as his painless but stiff limbs allowed.

His erect presence was breaking the waves of oncoming people. He looked into one face after another, all smiling at him for a short moment, but then passing by on the way to the river that seemed to draw them all toward its shores. Then a young man bumped into him, wearing a wetsuit and holding his left arm in his right hand. He dropped his arm and Nepomuk politely picked it up. The arm was wet and cold and had bite marks all along the forearm.

"Thanks, mate. Might still need it," the young man said before fixing his eyes onto the waters again.

A shiver ran down Nepomuk's spine, and he began to breathe heavily. Could it be true?

Nepomuk closed his eyes and focused with all his might onto the foggy memory.

"They gave me morphine."

The old man nodded.

"I was in hospital, not for very long, I don't think. I was in pain; that's why they gave me morphine. It numbed the pain, but it also made my wife disappear. My beautiful Blanka."

Nepomuk couldn't speak further. A different kind of pain usurped his senses now, a pain so deep and dolorous that no drug could have calmed it. He couldn't believe that he would never see his wife again. He saw her beautiful face smiling at him from behind the counter in their small bakery shop. She always tilted her head down slightly, as if watching him in secrecy, but she never turned her eyes away when he looked back at her. It had always made his stomach tingle when he caught her gaze, and he never quite understood how he could have been so lucky to have found her.

It was an extraordinary set of circumstances when they finally met. For years, it turned out, they had moved around the country, always missing each other by a few months. He had taken to the road after his apprenticeship as a baker and she had run away with a small touring theatre company, taking occasional jobs here and there to finance her daily life.

His final test to become a master baker was to make a baker's dozen of fruit loaves, all of equal size and quality, with dried redcurrants. He seasoned the dough with cardamom and cinnamon and decorated the bread with almond slivers. The crusts were perfect, the currents were still juicy in the white loaf, and he passed the test with full marks.

An hour later, he was selling the bread at the market. The world was at his feet, and he sold every item in record time. The last fruit loaf was purchased by the most beautiful woman he had ever seen. Until the end, Nepomuk thought it was this bread that had sealed the deal, although Blanka maintained that it was his sunny disposition that day. She returned the next day to buy another loaf and was disappointed to find that he hadn't made any more. He promised that he would have some the next day, just for her, if she returned. She did return, and she stayed.

Nepomuk wanted to scream, but his throat felt painfully swollen. Instead, he spun around as fast as his old limbs allowed and pushed his way against the never-ending stream of the recently deceased.

Further and further, he pushed and yet did not seem to make any distance between himself and the river. Where were all those people coming from?

"Blanka," he muttered under his breath until he was shouting her name into the dead faces, but no one answered, not even pausing to help him in his despair.

In the end, he stopped and cried like he had never cried before.

As if he hadn't moved at all, the old man was once again by his side.

"Is there no way back?" Nepomuk finally managed to croak. "All those stories always had the heroes return."

"That's why I'm still here. Unfortunately, I never read much, but one thing I know is that I won't cross that river."

Nepomuk stopped, exhausted. He couldn't be dead. There was still so much he needed to say, so many memories to be made.

"How long have you been here then?" he asked, desperate to find any clue about how to return from the dead. His daughter was getting married in four months and he had to walk her down the aisle.

"Time's a funny thing here. Could be fifty, could be one year or one hundred years."

"Are you saying that I could have died months ago?" yelled Nepomuk.

"Or years," the old man shrugged. "All I know is that I have walked along the shoreline for a very long time in both directions and always ended up back here. That, or this place is just the same everywhere you go."

Nepomuk spun around and looked in all directions. There was the river, about a hundred metres wide. Even though the surface seemed unmoving, a strong current appeared to flow underneath judging by the everchanging colours of green, brown, and grey. He did not see a ferry and wondered whether, even in the afterlife, passage only happened according to a schedule, maybe even with delays, depending on whether Charon, the ferryman, had overslept or felt a little under the weather. The other side of the river was deserted, as if none of the dead actually made it across.

Behind him was an empty plain that stretched with no end in sight. No tree or bush or rock or stone drew Nepomuk's view. The only thing he saw was the never-ending army of dead arriving from nowhere and making their way towards the shoreline.

But far away, along the river, he could see a mountain chain. "What is that?" he asked the old man.

"Never reached it; didn't even get closer."

"And what is on the other side of the river?"

"I told you, I have never, and I will never cross that damn river. I might not have read much in my lifetime, but I heard the stories of people being tortured for their sins."

"You sinned much then?" asked Nepomuk sarcastically.

"See, that's the thing: I can't remember. For all I know, I could have been the pope, or a gangster."

"Well, you don't look like either."

The old man looked down at his green clothes.

"Probably true, but that doesn't mean I haven't sinned."

Nepomuk gazed at the river again.

"I don't want to get tortured either," he said thoughtfully.

"Not a saint yourself then?"

"Who is?" grunted Nepomuk.

"A saint?"

"Ever seen one?"

The old man thought for a second, then shrugged.

Nepomuk bent down and sat on the dusty ground, something he hadn't done in probably forty years, since his son was a child. He felt his joints gnash and wondered whether he would ever get back up again. The old man joined him after some awkward stretches and a kind of sideways drop.

"Well, it doesn't seem like any of our earthly ailments disappear here either," judged Nepomuk.

"Had that gout for as long as I can think. At least it's not hurting anymore."

"So, you do remember something – from before?" asked Nepomuk.

"Sometimes I think I remember something, but then it slips away like a trout in a clear river."

"Maybe you were a fisherman?"

"Maybe. Do they wear this?" asked the old man and pointed at his jacket.

"Looks more like something a gardener or a forester would wear. Do you know anything about plants?"

"I don't think so, but I like daffodils."

They sat for a while watching the steady stream of dead people move around them. Someone started a brawl somewhere, but it did not spread; most people just passed around the troublemakers without seeming to see that anything was happening. After a while the troublemakers as well as any potential witnesses were gone.

A woman with a baby on her arm passed them. They looked as if they had been in a car accident. The baby was cooing, and its mother smiled tenderly; or at least this is what Nepomuk thought she was doing, as her head was smashed into smithereens on one side and the inside of her skull was now outside.

"Are they in pain?" asked Nepomuk.

"Were you in pain?" replied the old man.

"Yes."

"Are you in pain now?"

"No."

"There you go. They only look twisted, but when you look at them a little longer, they're actually alright. Not pretty, but alright."

Nepomuk lost all feeling for time. The light did not change, nor were there any clouds in the sky or wind in the air. The only thing that changed were the people around them. Despite more and more deceased making their way to the river, the crowd itself did not seem to grow, and when Nepomuk tried to keep track of someone to maybe catch a glimpse of the ferry, they seemed to vanish as soon as he lost the line of sight even for a moment.

"Has anyone ever met someone again that they knew from before?" he wondered aloud.

"Not that I know of. But then, I don't remember my own wife, or even if I had one." The old man had gotten up to see what Nepomuk was watching.

"You remember nothing from your life?"

"Maybe I do, but I wouldn't know whether they are memories or just wishful thinking."

"Do you remember your name?"

"No, but I like Humphrey."

"Really?" Nepomuk was amused for the first time.

"Yeah, like Humphrey Bogart."

"So, you do remember some things," exclaimed Nepomuk.

"I do? Who is Humphrey Bogart?"

"He was an actor, but he must've died more than sixty years ago."

"Do you think I am Humphrey Bogart?"

"I'm pretty sure you are not Humphrey Bogart."

"Maybe I met him here, then," mused the old man, somewhat disappointed.

"Maybe, or the things that you like are actually your memories. What else do you like?"

"I like ... I like gardens that don't look like gardens, I like to watch evening primroses go to sleep and to wake up to the smell of fresh bread."

"I was a baker," interrupted Nepomuk.

"You like bakers?" questioned the old man.

"No, but I remember that I *was* a baker."

"And what name do you like?"

"Nepomuk."

"Humphrey," the old man stretched his hand out. "Nice to meet you. So, it seems it's just you and me."

"Well, and the millions and billions of others."

"Yes, but no one ever stays, just you and me." Humphrey seemed to lighten up at that thought.

"Has anyone ever waited for someone?"

A thought, a desire, had emerged in Nepomuk. Maybe he could wait for Blanka, and they could make their way over the river together. Facing torture with a loved one seemed much more bearable.

Chapter 2

Nepomuk and Humphrey sat for a long while together and talked, Nepomuk about his memories and Humphrey about what he liked, which might have been memories or just hopes and dreams. If they were memories, then Humphrey had lived in a Victorian mansion with a crazy lady under the roof. He fancied that he had a wife called Emma and that his name might actually have been George, but he preferred Humphrey now. He also used to ride a beautiful black horse that ran away when he was a little boy but came back years later. Because none of his memories included any electronic items, Nepomuk assumed that Humphrey must have been dead for a while.

Nepomuk in turn told Humphrey how he met his wife Blanka, and the fruit loaf she loved so much.

"And then you eat it with lightly salted butter and honey," explained Nepomuk.

"That sounds lovely. Almost like something my dear Mama could have made, I imagine," responded Humphrey. "You know, I'm glad we found each other. This could be the beginning of a beautiful friendship. I felt like I was going crazy all by myself."

Nepomuk considered his words, as they were surrounded by the dead who arrived in droves by the minute.

"You never spoke to anyone else?"

"Why, I did, all the time. But they always seem, you know, a little cuckoo. Neither here nor there, not knowing where they are or what has happened to them. For a moment, I was afraid you'd turn out like them, but then you tried to run in the opposite direction of the river, and I knew you were different."

Nepomuk smiled. He was glad he was different, that he remembered; some things, at least. The good things.

But as he sat there and thought about his memories, he could only clearly recount three. Selling Blanka his fruit loaf, the birth of his son in the middle of the night, and the birth of his daughter on their kitchen floor. There were a few other more vague memories, like his son losing a tooth in a bicycle accident, and some things that were more a feeling than a memory.

Monday mornings, after a long day at the bakery on Sundays, when the house was still quiet as the sun was coming up, lying in bed with Blanka's head resting on his chest, her finger tracing the curve of his ear. He tried to recall more of these mornings. Did he reciprocate her tenderness? Did they kiss or make love?

As Nepomuk tried to recollect this memory, he realized he ought to be able to remember so much more. Where did they live? Where did his children go to school? How old were they?

And then all his emotions broke out again.

"What's the matter?" asked Humphrey when Nepomuk leaped up, spasmodically sobbing and walking away again without moving from the spot.

"I can't remember their names," howled Nepomuk.

"Whose?"

"My children. I can't remember."

"Which names do you like?" asked Humphrey in a desperate attempt to make him stop.

"It doesn't work like that. They have names, they are real. It's not something I can make up, like Humphrey."

Deep down, Nepomuk understood he'd hurt the old man, but he didn't care. He knew he had two children, a son and a daughter, and they deserved to be remembered by their father. It was one thing knowing that they were probably grieving his death and that he wasn't there with them to make more memories, but it was an entirely different thing to not remember the memories that they had made together during his lifetime, and to forget something as important as their names. Names that Blanka and he had probably carefully chosen over nine months. Or had they used the grandparents' names? What were his parents' names?

The only name he could remember was Blanka.

"What time is it?" asked Nepomuk, still walking.

"I don't know," said Humphrey, who hadn't moved at all.

"How long since I arrived here?"

"I don't know."

"Blanka! Blanka!" shouted Nepomuk. Maybe it had been a few years already and she was here, one of the millions, and he only had to find her.

If only he could find her, everything would be alright.

"Blanka!" Nepomuk shouted again, and he felt he was going crazy as he pushed through a group of people who were sprinkled in something that might have been the dust of a collapsed building.

He stopped, exhausted, then looked at Humphrey, who had sat down again a while ago.

"No one ever paused to find their loved ones?"

19

"No one."

Nepomuk's head was racing. If Blanka had arrived at Epipedo, he had to find her.

"Where do people come from?"

"Well," Humphrey cleared his throat. "That is an awkward question for a grown man with two children. But okay. You know, when a man and a woman love each other very much—" he began.

"No, I mean how do people get here?"

"Ah, I don't know. How did you get here?"

Nepomuk racked his brain, but no matter how hard he focused on the fog of his last memory, he could not come up with anything. It was as if there was nothing to remember. There hadn't been a light or a voice and certainly no one who had guided him. He had just woken up here.

"Hey, how did you get here?" Nepomuk asked a random stranger who was clutching his heart.

But all he got in return was a serene smile before the man continued his path to the shore.

"Excuse me. Do you know where we are?"

"The Summerland, dear. Come," answered an old lady in a lacy nightdress.

Nepomuk did not follow her.

"I'm telling you, they are all a little cuckoo," shrugged Humphrey.

"Where are you going?" insisted Nepomuk, placing a hand on someone's shoulder.

"To meet my ancestors." And on they walked.

"Where are you from?" he asked another person.

"Pretoria."

"Wait, why don't you stay here?"

"Alright."

Nepomuk looked in surprise down to Humphrey, who beamed back up.

The person looked at both of them expectantly but then something invisible drew their attention and on they walked to the shore.

"No, wait. Why do they all walk like lemmings to that river?" scowled Nepomuk, and on he went asking random people where they were from, where they were now and where they were heading.

The answers were as different as the people he asked. The only thing in common was that each gave their answers with certainty.

"I'm telling you, there's only you and me. No one ever stays and no one ever goes back," said Humphrey, who was still sitting on the ground next to him, no matter how much Nepomuk moved around the crowd.

He was desperate, but Humphrey was right. They were alone amongst millions. No one cared for the person next to them. Everyone seemed to exist in their own bubble, whether they believed they were in the Summerland, Nirvana, or Paradise. It seemed that whatever the person wanted this place to be was exactly what they got; or at least believed they had got. Nepomuk pondered whether they all saw the river or whether it looked different to different people. And then he questioned why he saw the River Styx. He had never been religious and always insisted that there was nothing whatsoever after death. You just ceased to exist in body and soul: no paradise, no afterlife or rebirth.

As he stared down at the dusty ground, trampled and compacted to hard rock, he remembered, or rather felt, that as a teenager he had been intrigued by the Greek myths, but he certainly never believed that they were true.

Some legs came past his view, and suddenly there was a baby lying on the ground, butt naked and seemingly trying to grip something with its hands and legs. It wasn't crying or in any distress; it was simply there and in the unfortunate position that it had died before it had learned to walk.

Nepomuk felt an urge to pick it up, but before he could make a step, someone else took it into their arms and carried it down to the river. And for the first time, he was curious about what lay on the other side of the stream. Surely no one would torture an innocent baby over there.

He made a few steps towards the shore.

"Where are you going?" shouted Humphrey, and when Nepomuk turned back he had actually moved away from his companion.

"Nowhere. I was just wondering," said Nepomuk.

"Why, for crying out loud. I can't hear you now; you're too far away!" cried Humphrey.

"I said," and with this Nepomuk tried to walk back to Humphrey, "I'm not going anywhere."

"Why did you go closer to that damn river?" asked Humphrey. "There is no way back."

Humphrey was right; no matter how many steps Nepomuk took towards him, he did not get closer.

"What is this?"

"You can only get closer to the river, but not walk away from it," explained Humphrey.

Nepomuk looked around. Just to test it, he took one step backward. And indeed, this way he could increase the distance from the old man.

"Stop doing that! I'm not going to follow you," threatened Humphrey.

"What are we going to do now?" shouted Nepomuk.

"I don't know. Tell me something more of your life," the old man shouted back.

Nepomuk sat down. "I've told you everything I remember."

"Then tell me what you like."

Nepomuk thought for a while. "I like Monday mornings."

"Have you gone crazy?"

"No, I really do. No one buys Sunday rolls on a Monday."

"Why would they? They'd be hard by the next Sunday. What else do you like?"

"I like sleeping in a freshly made bed. I like the dreamlike sounds of a violin, and people whistling in the streets. I like the change of the seasons."

"Oh, I like that too. Have you ever seen an ash tree in autumn – I mean, really seen it?"

"Maybe."

"It's like having a sunset outside your window every hour of the day."

The two men sat in silence for a moment, each thinking about their favourite things.

"Do you ever eat anything here?" asked Nepomuk after a minute or maybe a day.

"Why? Are you hungry?" asked the old man.

"No, not really. I was just thinking that I would like to taste a sweet cheese strudel."

"Sounds scrumptious. But there's no food here, or beds or toilets. Probably because you're never hungry or sleepy or need to spend a penny."

Nepomuk thought about this. Nothing here was welcoming and even if he knew he could find Blanka in this overrun desert, it would be a challenge. But how could he guarantee not to miss her? She had no reason to wait and would probably take the ferry just like everyone else. Maybe on the other side there was someone who could tell him how to find someone or at least message someone. Weren't there supposed to be gods or nymphs or something? Mercury; no, that was a Roman god. He wished he had paid more attention at school. But who knew: Roman or Greek, they might be the same thing after all, or nothing, or whatever the seeker desired.

"Why don't we at least have a look and see if there is someone at the shore who can answer some questions. We don't need to pass over, just look," suggested Nepomuk finally.

"Over my dead body!" shouted Humphrey.

"That's a deal then, seeing that you are already dead," grinned Nepomuk.

"When hell freezes over, then," came the response.

"Alright, let's go and have a look how cold it is down there. What do you have to lose?"

Humphrey turned away and took several demonstrative steps away from Nepomuk, which did not lead him anywhere.

"Oh, come on. Humphrey, just to the shore!" shouted Nepomuk.

"Why, hello there, might I tell you you're a bit of jam?" Humphrey complimented a lady in an open hospital gown who looked as though she had lost her fight for life to cancer.

Her serene look was briefly shadowed before she moved on without a word.

"Oi, fancy a soccer match?" he hustled a man in a sports outfit. "No? Football? Cricket? Croquet?"

"Come on, old chap. I'll take the challenge if you come with me to the shore. What's keeping you here anyway?" asked Nepomuk, watching the old man in his anguish.

Now, it was Humphrey who was jumbling between the masses without moving anywhere and Nepomuk saw how ridiculous and sad it looked to try and walk away from the river; like trying to avoid fate.

"Do you really want to spend all eternity here with no one to speak to?" asked Nepomuk.

"You are evil!" shouted Humphrey as he turned around with tears running down his face. "Don't you think I know how it is being here? Merely existing with no one to share this nothingness? This hell?"

Nepomuk wished he could go back to Humphrey and give him a hug. "Maybe this is your purgatory, and it is up to you to decide when to leave it," Nepomuk suggested.

"I don't want to be here anymore. I just don't want to be. I don't have any memories to cheer me up, no one stays with me, there is nothing to enjoy. What's the point in being dead?" cried Humphrey.

"Come on then, we'll cross the river together and see what lies on the other side. It can't be worse than this! And at least you've got me," pleaded Nepomuk.

Humphrey looked pained.

"Oh, alright then," he sniffled finally and walked reluctantly toward Nepomuk and closer to the dreaded river.

They slowly but steadily approached the shore, where the water rushed silently in eternally changing colours. Nepomuk could feel his heart racing – at least, he thought it was racing; he wasn't sure whether it was actually still beating. He could still see nothing on the river or beyond. There was no ferry, bridge, or tunnel, no one was swimming across or getting their feet wet, and yet people seemed to disappear.

"They really don't make it easy to cross, huh?" said Humphrey, staring wide-eyed across the river.

"Maybe people swim and it's some sort of invisibility water," mused Nepomuk.

"I'd rather swim than get on board with this fella," said Humphrey, looking frightened.

"What?" asked Nepomuk.

"Charon. I mean if we swam, we might meet a lovely nymph."

"You see Charon?"

"Yes, he's right there."

"Where?"

"Right in front of us. His barge is almost touching your foot."

Nepomuk tried to take a step back.

"What's up with you? You know that doesn't work. You really can't see him?" asked Humphrey.

"No," answered Nepomuk, and he felt panic closing his throat again.

"Maybe you have to spend your share of time alone in Epipedo."

"Are you saying you'd leave me here now?" accused Nepomuk. He was surprised that, after all the drama, Humphrey seemed eager to go aboard Charon's ferry.

"Well, I thought we were going together," said Humphrey.

"But I don't see the ferry."

"Maybe it's only one person per fare?" suggested Humphrey and looked quizzically to some invisible ferryman.

"Maybe. It's okay. I'll see you on the other side," said Nepomuk wistfully.

"Are you sure?"

"Yes," nodded Nepomuk.

"And you are not duping me?"

"Why would I?"

"Well, you're still hoping to find your wife, so maybe you're glad to get rid of me."

"I promise, I'm not lying."

"But you are still looking for your wife?"

"Of course I am. But how would I find her here?" Nepomuk looked back at the oncoming deceased. "I reckon there must be something on the other side that is more promising than this."

And with this, Nepomuk glanced back across the river and stumbled backwards, only he remained where he was, as he looked into the furrowed face of the ferryman. Charon stood unmoving and unblinking on his barge, cloaked from head to toe and with a wide-brimmed hat. His gaze penetrated Nepomuk and reached far beyond him with eyes that lacked the natural glimmer of a living being.

With shaking fingers, Nepomuk searched for the coin in his pocket and finally approached the barge with the obolus stretched out in front of him.

"For my friend and me," croaked Nepomuk and nodded to Humphrey.

"So, now you see him?"

"Oh yes, I do. Come on," whispered Nepomuk without turning his eyes away from the ferryman.

Nepomuk and Humphrey clambered into the barge and huddled on a wooden bench as far away from Charon as possible. He turned around without looking at them and punted away from the shore.

Chapter 3

THE RIVER WAS SMOOTH, like a mountain lake. Only Charon's pole splashed quietly, and, to Nepomuk's discomfort, the disturbed water swirled red amid the river-green and clung to the pole like blood.

"Why is there no one else on the river? There should be millions being ferried across every minute," remarked Humphrey, who was gazing with a morbid fascination over the side of the boat.

"I think they are, but somehow everything appears to exist to the individual's expectation," explained Nepomuk.

He was still unsure about the laws of this place, but it seemed to him that everyone got what they thought they would get. He wondered whether he should start hoping for Paradise, and worried because he couldn't shake off Humphrey's talk about torture.

"Do you think we could ask him what happens next?" asked Humphrey, nodding to the back of Charon.

Nepomuk shrugged and felt the words clumping inside his mouth. He truly was not a nice-looking fella.

"Go on; maybe he's seen your Blanka already," prompted Humphrey.

Nepomuk gave him an upset look. He didn't like it when people used private information to extract an action.

"Excuse me," said Nepomuk finally and raised a hand. "Could you tell me whether there is someone on the other side to leave a message for my wife?"

Charon did not move apart from his rhythmic punting.

"Her name is Blanka. You might have met her already."

Nepomuk reached out to tug on Charon's cloak to get his attention when Humphrey suddenly started moaning.

"What?" hissed Nepomuk, his heart almost jumping out of his mouth.

"Oh no. Oh no. No, no, no." Humphrey buried his face in his hands.

"What happened? Did you forget something?" asked Nepomuk, concerned.

"On the contrary. I remember." Humphrey emerged with tears in his eyes and frantically scurried away from the edge of the barge, linking his arm under Nepomuk's.

"You mean actual memories?"

"Yes, all of it!" sobbed Humphrey.

As Nepomuk investigated the old man's face he was astounded to see it change in age from a young man in his early twenties, to middle age, to a child (which was quite worrying to look at as his body remained that of a grown man), and back to his old self. The only constant was the sorrow that showed on his face. And as he observed this peculiar transformation, he too remembered everything.

His children were called Marek and Luella. They hadn't used their grandparents' names as they wanted their children to have their own identities. They lived in Pilsen, and his daughter was supposed to get married to Nicolai on May 27th. He had been losing weight for the past three years. At first, he had joked that he would have no problems getting his beach body that summer, but after another winter he knew that something wasn't right. He still maintained his sunny disposition and hid his tiredness and his stomach cramps from everyone. The doctors always gave him a clean bill of health until they finally found the tumour on his pancreas.

Blanka had insisted on him going to the hospital after she found that his hands were ice cold, and his lips were turning blue during a relaxed stroll in the Botanical Gardens on Easter Monday. He insisted that there was nothing wrong and that he'd had a full check-up only a few months ago. But he gave in to give her peace of mind. At the hospital, he was surprised when Blanka explicitly told the doctors to check his stomach. Apparently, he hadn't been as successful as he had thought in hiding his ailments.

He read his diagnosis alone in his hospital room after the doctor had left his patient notes with him. It took him another two days before he told Blanka.

The tumour was inoperable. The only option was chemotherapy to shrink it and loosen its grip around the organ. They told him about the side effects and the slim chances that it would work. Blanka and he even discussed not doing anything and letting the cancer take its course in the hopes of having at least some final happy weeks or maybe months if they were lucky. He might even make it to Luella's wedding. But Nepomuk clung to the hope that he could have more than just a few happy months if he endured chemotherapy now.

The first week was bearable but with every dose the side effects got worse. By the end of the month, he had been admitted to hospital for stronger pain medication. In the end, he was barely conscious, and whilst the doctors thought they had his pain under control, he was simply not able to tell them or show them otherwise. But the pain was still there, not precisely located but rather all through his body, from his bones to his skin, a dull all-encompassing ache.

He was also aware of the people entering his room. Even though his eyes had dulled and were dry because he couldn't close them completely anymore, he could still tell if it was Blanka, Marek or Luella. He always tried to breathe as calmly as possible when they were there to give them peace. The last few days, he knew death was coming and he held on to the world, in his thoughts at least, for as long as they were there. Come night, he relaxed and searched with his clouded senses for the bodyless presence of someone to take his hand and guide him over. And every morning he awoke in the hospital room, he tried his best again to stay alive just to be with his family. And then, he had woken up in Epipedo, remembering as little as he did on his last day that he had been in the hospital bed.

The barge had passed the middle of the river now and Nepomuk wondered whether this was what lay on the other side: the memories of everything of their past lives. If so, then this came close to torture – at least if you left a life behind that had brought you joy.

"Do you want to tell me about your life?" asked Nepomuk finally, trying to avoid thinking about all the things he had lost.

Humphrey shook his head and instead cried unconsolably.

The barge glided onto the shore on the other side and Humphrey scrambled to alight. He was in such haste that he pushed by Charon, got tangled in the ferryman's clothes and fell face first into the gravel.

"Terribly sorry," mumbled Nepomuk as he squeezed by, but Charon did not seem to be disturbed. As soon as Nepomuk had left, he pushed away again to continue his eternal task.

"What's the matter with you?" asked Nepomuk and gave the old man a hand.

"I drowned," exclaimed Humphrey. "I drowned trying to catch a trout. Fell in from a rowing boat. What was I thinking? Clearly not much. Wasn't thinking at all. Why would I want to go fishing? Such a stupid idea. Gone fishing? Well, quite obviously."

"Maybe you were hungry," suggested Nepomuk.

"No, I wasn't. I was bloody demented, was I. Lived in a high-security care home for the past ten years. Had terrible fits of rage because no one could understand me. And how could they? Didn't even know meself who I was? And this nurse, Betty, she'd always come and read bloody Jane Austen romance novels to me when they had drugged me up. She fell asleep watching a film, *Casablanca*, was it, and I was just enough myself to climb down that ash tree in front of me window. I'm surprised I didn't kick the bucket at that manoeuvre. Well, didn't make it far after, I can tell you that."

Nepomuk was highly amused at this outburst and change in character.

"And what about your wife, Emma?" asked Nepomuk as he sat down next to Humphrey.

"Emma? Me wife was called Clementine, but I used to call her Clemmie. She was the sweetest, most patient and kindest woman in the whole wide world."

Nepomuk nodded, smiling.

"She killed herself because of me. Couldn't bear the way I was going."

Humphrey began crying again, and when Nepomuk gave him a hug, he clung to him like a small child.

As they sat like this, Nepomuk took in their surroundings. They were on a plain again that looked just like the other side.

Compacted sand, trampled from millions of feet, a mountain chain in the back, but somehow it wasn't nearly as crowded. He wondered whether everybody arrived on the same shore or whether some people were lucky enough to be transported straight to the Elysian Fields.

Again, there was nothing to see on this side of the river, but the people who did arrive on their shore often seemed just as shaken as they were, and a number needed to sit down and cry. Some actually lay down and seemed to take a nap. Others got up and wandered about for a while before deciding on a direction. Some walked in groups, enjoying the company and conversation, and others walked in solitude.

To Nepomuk's disappointment, again there was no one who seemed to know what they were supposed to do. At least it seemed they weren't restricted in their movement anymore, people talked with each other, and were physical intact.

"They could have put a lemonade stand here," joked someone passing by.

"I used to sell lemonade as a kid," said another.

"We'd need a supermarket first," said a third.

"A lemon tree would be enough," said the first.

"But what about water and honey?"

And on they walked.

"My Clemmie used to make a delicious sweet cheese strudel. You would have liked it."

Humphrey reappeared from Nepomuk's arms and wiped his nose on his sleeve.

"I'm sure I would have," smiled Nepomuk.

"What do we do now?" asked Humphrey.

"I don't know. Seems like we are all still left to our own devices."

"I wonder if I could go to sleep and find everything good again when I woke up," pondered Humphrey.

"Since everyone seems to be doing what they like, I can't see why you couldn't sleep."

With that, Humphrey curled up into a ball. "You know what? I think my gout has gone."

Shortly after, Humphrey was indeed fast asleep, snoring peacefully.

Nepomuk, on the other hand, felt restless. He got up and walked back to the river to see if he could talk to Charon again, but just like before, he couldn't see the ferryman or his barge, only people who appeared on the shore. Maybe things only appeared when you were ready for them and needed them. And since he didn't need to return, the ferry remained inaccessible to him.

He helped up a woman who had fallen to her knees, presumably when she disembarked. At first, he assumed she was an old lady, but when she was on her feet again, she proved to be a young woman with a long braid.

"Thank you so much," she said and smiled at him.

"Not to worry," he replied.

"Maybe you could tell me where to go next?" asked the woman.

"Terribly sorry, I also just got here," answered Nepomuk.

"Oh, well. I guess I'll have a look around then."

"Where would you like to go?" asked Nepomuk

"Somewhere nice. You know, when I was young, I visited Neuschwanstein Castle. It was like a fairy tale, up on a mountaintop amid a dark pine forest. I'd always wanted to go back again to see it in winter. Imagine how beautiful it must look when everything is covered in glistening white snow."

Nepomuk had seen pictures of the castle and agreed that it must be a sight to behold.

"You could come with me," she suggested.

"I'd love to, but I'm waiting for someone." Nepomuk could see the disappointment in her eyes. "I'm sure there are plenty of people who'd love to join you."

"Are you waiting for your girlfriend?"

Nepomuk looked a little surprised. "My wife."

"Oh, you look too young to be married."

Now, Nepomuk was genuinely astonished, as he was seventy-seven.

"Never mind. Do you know whether I could get some food anywhere? Just some provisions for the road. It looks like it might be a long way."

"I don't think you need any food here."

"No, I know. But it's such a nice thing to have a picnic on the side of the road."

"I'm sorry, but I really don't know."

"I'll see what I can find," said the young woman, "and I hope you find your wife."

"Thank you," smiled Nepomuk, and with that she began walking in a direction that a small group of others had already chosen.

He walked back to Humphrey, who was still sleeping, now stretched out like a starfish. A little away, a group of rambunctious young men were running, and jumping and bumping into each other, as if they had no care in the world – or rather in the underworld. As he looked on, one of them took a run-up towards the others and then jumped about two metres high right over their heads and landed as light as a butterfly. Nepomuk was still holding his breath when the rest of the group passed as if nothing had happened.

This place was truly full of surprises. If it didn't look so uninviting, Nepomuk thought this could be like Paradise, where every wish could come true.

A loud yawn drew his attention away from the disappearing group.

"How long did I sleep?" asked Humphrey.

"Maybe five minutes," guessed Nepomuk.

"Really? I feel like I had a full night's sleep. Who would have thought that this gravel could feel like a feather bed?" Humphrey pushed the ground around him, which dented in as if it were a feather bed. "I feel like a new man. You know what? I'll take a leaf out of your book and see if I can find Clemmie. I feel like I have a lot to apologize for."

"Really? You think you can find her?" asked Nepomuk, who had a niggling doubt about ever finding Blanka again.

"I have to try," said Humphrey, brushing the dust from his clothes. "I assume you'll stay?"

"Yes," said Nepomuk weighing his chances in his heart.

"Thank you for setting me free," said Humphrey and gave Nepomuk a sincere and bone-crushing hug. Somehow, his appearance had settled to about twenty years younger, with broad shoulders and a full head of dusty blond hair.

"You did it all yourself," Nepomuk squeezed out.

"I hope we see each other again and I get to meet your Blanka. Got to go now, Clemmie has some fifteen years' lead on me."

"Take care, Humphrey!" Nepomuk shouted after the not-so-old man.

"Me name's John!" he shouted as he waved a final good-bye.

Chapter 4

NEPOMUK SAT DOWN AND watched the shore. With all his might he willed that the next person to appear would be Blanka, but he recognized no one and no one recognized him. Then he thought that if wishes did come true in this place, he shouldn't wish to see Blanka, as he might cause her untimely death. Instead, he wished for the sun to set so he could sleep, but the light didn't fade. Was it the sun that lit this place? Nepomuk couldn't see any light source in the sky or anywhere else.

He shimmied around to get more comfortable. After a few skids, the ground began to feel like a sofa cushion. He again observed the people arriving on the shore, but instead of wishing for Blanka to appear he delved into his memories.

When he was little, his family kept a couple of pigs and chickens behind the house. One day, his mother had not closed the pen properly and one of the pigs escaped. The whole family got together to catch the runaway, who seemed to enjoy this freedom and did everything to avoid being penned up again. Finally, they cornered it. His mother guarded the only exit through a narrow passage between the houses, whilst Nepomuk and his brother slowly but surely approached it to guide it back into the pen. Instead of turning right, though, the pig took a run at their mother, who stood bravely in her spot without budging. Unfortunately, she also wore an ankle-length dress, as was the fashion of the time, which spanned her open legs, and the pig in its despair dived right between her legs. The dress caught on the pig's head and their mother flopped onto the pig's back with her head near the animal's muddy bottom. Just like that, his mother took a ride on the blindfolded pig all along the street before she slipped off near the next corner. Eventually, the pig was chased back by a policeman who had come to the rescue after hearing his mother's screams for help.

Nepomuk found himself laughing at this memory. He had been ten years old then, and it was a story that Luella had requested over and over again when she was the same age.

When he was about six years old, he had tried to slaughter a chicken as he had seen his grandfather do. Unfortunately, he had not been strong enough and tortured the poor bird by repeatedly hitting it with a hatchet on the neck. His grandfather rushed into the shed with a raised shotgun, expecting a fox. He gave him a telling off and released the animal from its agony by breaking its neck with a swift turn of his hands.

Then, Nepomuk remembered the first time he saw his parents. His body was being squeezed by his mother's birth contractions and someone placed a hand on his head to catch him when he slipped out. It was cold and he screamed as everything was rough and strange; the noises were much louder and the lights much brighter. But then he was embraced warmly and heard familiar voices. He squinted and saw his mother's blurred nose and the shape of his father's face behind her. He remembered that he hoped she would never let him go and that he could stay in her warm arms forever.

Amazed at these clear memories of his own birth, Nepomuk wondered whether he could remember anything before this. And indeed, he did. Similar to his mother's warm arms, he was encompassed by a warm orb, softly stroked by its palpitations; he heard his parents' voices from a distance and noticed the shadow of a small hand on the outside, which must have been his brother's.

Nepomuk was abruptly pulled out of his cocoon of cosy memories when a girl collapsed close enough to him that he could not ignore her weeping. On the other side of the river, everyone looked as they had when they died and on many you could see the scars with which life had marked them. On this side of the river, everyone looked unharmed, but now their memories haunted them. By now, he had seen so many dead people arrive who cried and wept, who remained immobile for a small eternity, but also many who smiled and even laughed before moving on, so Nepomuk didn't find the woman's behaviour unusual.

So instead of being thoughtful and offering her a kind word, he lay down to reminisce in his own memories. He found that the gravel was indeed very comfortable, and even though he was not tired or felt the need to sleep, he closed his eyes and drifted off into his past life.

When he arose again after having re-lived his memories from about twenty years, the woman was still there. She sat with her legs clutched tight to her body and her head thumping rhythmically down on her knees.

"Are you alright?" asked Nepomuk finally.

When he didn't get an answer, he got up to sit next to her. "Are you okay?" he asked again.

The woman stopped bumping her head up and down. "No," came her response.

"Good memories?" asked Nepomuk.

"No," came the reply again from the depth of her curled-up body.

Apparently, Nepomuk was wrong when he thought that only good memories would haunt people here. "Do you want to talk about them?"

The woman was now completely still. "I just want to forget," she whispered eventually.

Nepomuk nodded knowingly even though he had no idea what she might be remembering that was so terrifying.

"Do you want me to go away?" he asked.

A soft shake let Nepomuk know that he was invited to stay a little longer.

Nepomuk told the woman about Humphrey, who thought he was George, only to remember that his name was John. He tried to colour his memories of his old companion as brightly as possible to show how even a terrible life on Earth could be the beginning of a happy end here in the afterlife.

"And what are you waiting for?" asked the women without looking up.

"I'm waiting for my wife. Her name is Blanka."

"Tell me about her."

Nepomuk told her about the loaf of bread and their Monday mornings, though he left out the specific details that he now remembered. Then the birth of their two children, and how Marek had lost his tooth.

By the time he told her how he had toppled over the neighbour's fence with a ladder trying to pick apples and then being chased up the tree by the neighbour's dogs, she had lain down. She was still curled up, but Nepomuk could see her face for the first time. She looked older than Nepomuk had expected but that may have been because the memories still had her in their grip.

"More," she whispered. Her eyes kept on staring straight ahead.

"Once, I must have been twelve or thirteen, my brother and I played a prank on a local man who would always spend hours on the public toilet. Where I grew up, many houses didn't have their own toilets yet and the public one was still a thunderbox – you know, just a beam with a hole behind it. The shack around was open on the bottom so that you could see whether it was occupied. Well, we had just slaughtered our pig and had a bucket full of blood, so me and my brother used this chance. My brother got our grandfather's shotgun and we sneaked up behind the thunderbox where this man – Janek Jezek was his name – sat again, already for an hour. No one knew what he was doing there for so long. Anyway, my brother shot into the air, and I splashed the bucket of blood under the thunderbox and onto Janek's backside. A second later he ran, his trousers still hanging around his ankles, through the streets, screaming 'They shot me in the butt, they shot me in the butt!'" Nepomuk chuckled at his own story.

"How old are you?" the woman asked when Nepomuk fell silent.

"Seventy-seven," he answered, a little surprised. "How old are you?"

"Twenty-two. When did you die?"

Nepomuk almost said yesterday but remembered that this didn't make sense where they were. "In May, 2017," he answered instead.

The woman nodded.

"What?" asked Nepomuk.

"Nothing; I just needed to put your story in perspective. Never heard the word *thunderbox* before."

Nepomuk smirked. He could see how the existence of a long drop must sound positively medieval to young people. Even his own children, who were more than a decade older than this woman, thought it funny.

"How did you die?" the women inquired further.

"Cancer."

"Do you remember when it happened?"

"I was pretty out of it on morphine."

At this the woman gave a sad smile.

"Funny, as now I even remember being in my mother's womb and being born."

"I remember that too," said the woman after a while. "That was nice. About the only nice memory I have."

She began to cry again, but this time in silence. Her tears ran freely over her cheek and wet the ground.

"When and how did you die, if I may ask?"

"Overdose, Christmas 2021."

"2021?" Nepomuk sat up straighter and scanned the shoreline with new interest. He'd been here for four and a half years already.

"You're still looking out for her?" The woman finally sat up and looked around for the first time since she'd arrived.

"Yes," said Nepomuk and got to his feet to be able to see further.

"That's really sweet. What did she look like?"

Nepomuk paused. In his mind he saw Blanka as a young woman with long dark hair and brown eyes. He smiled as he let her face pass through the years.

"She had shoulder-length hair. It used to be brown but at the end it had plenty of grey. She mostly wore it in a ponytail, but some strands always framed her face. She had this habit of combing it behind her ear with her fingers. Her eyes always smiled, and even when she frowned, her wrinkles gave her true nature away. Her favourite colour was cornflower blue, and her favourite play was Shakespeare's *A Midsummer Night's Dream*. She used to act in a travelling theatre company before we opened our bakery. She liked to read, especially Brecht. She insisted on reading his plays and poems to the kids at night as she wanted them to grow up as well-rounded people."

"Did it work?"

"I think so, though neither of them did anything in the arts."

She fell silent again, every now and then wiping tears away.

Nepomuk felt sorry for her but also didn't know how to console her. After all, they were pretty much strangers and he could have been her father; heck, even her grandfather.

But that gave him an idea. He thought about how he had consoled Luella when she had broken up with her first boy-friend, something that was not really comparable to finding yourself dead after an overdose, but nonetheless one of the biggest heartaches someone could go through. Instead of coaxing her to talk to him, he'd stick around and continue doing things around her. Bit by bit, he'd ask her to help him here and there until she was interested enough to ask questions about what he was doing. Then, it was only a matter of time until Luella would open up to him and all he had to do was be there and be ready to listen.

Nepomuk looked around to come up with something he could do. This turned out to be difficult as there was nothing. He ran his fingers across the ground trying to find something and came upon a stone. He turned it around in his hands. There was nothing remarkable about it. It was some sort of amalgamation of sand, granite, and larger bits of quartz in dif-ferent colours that gave it a colourless appearance. It was rough yet soft and bits crumbled off it and ran through his fingers like water. He finally had the idea to pretend he was making bread.

He scraped across the flat surface and pushed together the thin layer of loose sand. The more he did it, the easier it became until he had a large enough heap to form a loaf. He pretended that the sand was his flour and let it run through his finger to loosen it and crumble up any lumps. The more he did it, the bigger his gestures became, as if he were portraying a baker on stage. He picked up a pinch of dust and drizzled it as salt into his dough. Then he did the same with somewhat coarser sand that became his yeast.

He knew she had started watching him, albeit covertly, but this was the first step. Now, he gave his dry ingredients a good stir and formed a mound in which he pressed a hollow. Then, he picked up the stone again and pretended that it was an egg, which he cracked and dropped expertly with only one hand into the nest-shaped flour. He discarded the eggshells with an ostentatious flick of the wrist and propelled it over his shoulder. Finally, he got up and walked to the river. He needed some lukewarm water and even his inspired imagination could not see how adding more dry sand to his dough could be interpreted as any form of liquid.

For a moment he looked at the green river and remembered how it clung blood-red to the ferryman's pole, but there was no better substitute available. Gingerly, he immersed his hands into the water and was surprised that it came out crystal clear as he held it in the hollow of his cupped hands.

Carefully, he walked back to his workstation and poured the tepid water on top of his other ingredients. He sat back down and began to knead.

"What are you doing?" asked the woman finally.

Nepomuk smiled without looking up.

"I'm making a simple Christmas bread," he replied as he picked up the sand-dough, which had surprisingly formed into an elastic lump. He smashed it back onto the ground and kneaded it some more, hoping that the reference to Christmas did not trigger an adverse reaction in her.

"Could you pass me a handful of raisins?" he asked and pointed to some of the smaller gravel pieces lying abound.

Somewhat confused, the woman pointed to the little stones.

"Yes, a whole handful."

She collected the gravel around her in her hand. When it wasn't enough, she got up to collect some more until she had the required handful.

"Normally, I would have added some glazed cherries and apricots, but I'm short on ingredients here," he said when she dropped the raisins onto the dough so Nepomuk could work them in.

"I think I can find some," she responded and wandered off, picking more stones off the ground.

When she came back, she presented him with another handful of orange and dark red smooth, shimmering stones.

"These are some top ingredients. I'm a bit embarrassed now that I only used water and not warm milk," complimented Nepomuk.

"I'm sure it will taste good," she replied.

Nepomuk gave the dough another round of good whacking before he pulled a handkerchief out of his back pocket to cover it.

"What do we do now?" asked the woman.

"We wait for it to rise. A good bread takes time."

"My name's Enya," she finally said and pulled her chin up a little defiantly.

"I'm Nepomuk."

Chapter 5

"I REMEMBER WALKING HOME one night and there was this smell of freshly made bread in the air. It was really nice and welcoming. So, I sat down until the sun came up. People thought I was begging for money, and someone gave me a few coins. I bought two small bread rolls when the bakery opened. They were the best thing I had ever eaten, still warm inside and with sunflower seeds on top."

Nepomuk smiled at Enya's retelling of this experience.

"Wait until you've tried this bread, although I shouldn't promise too much since I didn't have milk."

"How are you going to bake it though?" asked Enya.

"Just like we made this dough: with a lot of experience and some imagination."

"Rather a lot of imagination."

Nepomuk got up and began drawing the outline of a stone oven into the soil. It wasn't big, but he included all the details he could remember. The double row of bricks that formed a cave-like ceiling, the chimney with a little iron roof so that the rain was kept out – not that it seemed to ever rain here, but too much moisture in the oven and the crusts wouldn't become nice and crisp. Then, he drew the wrought-iron door and even included the baroque letters of the maker, JG, on it.

At last, he drew the outline of a wooden bread paddle next to the oven.

"There. This looks like a nice little oven for our bread."

For the first time, Enya smiled, though Nepomuk wasn't sure whether she was genuinely happy or just going along with the old man's fantasy.

"I think it's time to tend to our dough again. There is one more thing we need to do." Nepomuk sat back down and carefully lifted his handkerchief.

The clump of sand, stones and water looked amazingly real when Nepomuk began separating it into three equal-sized balls to form long strands. It felt and smelled exactly like bread dough. Even the gravel and little stones they had added as raisins and glazed cherries and apricots looked soft and juicy.

Nepomuk began braiding the dough, carefully securing the ends and tucking them under to form a nice oval-shaped loaf. Enya watched him intently.

"Fetch the paddle," he said when he had given the top a light dusting with sand as he would have done with the yolk of an egg.

Enya turned but then didn't move and simply stared behind him. Nepomuk looked around and stood up in astonishment.

"Holy Moly," Nepomuk exclaimed at the fully formed albeit smaller version of his old bakery oven that stood on the plains.

He walked around it and placed a hand on the bricks. It was warm. In fact, it seemed the perfect temperature for bread.

"Here, put the loaf on the paddle," he said and picked up the paddle that was now also lying on the ground.

Enya picked up the braid and carefully slipped it onto the paddle before opening the oven door.

"Careful!"

Enya gave a shriek as she pulled her hand off the hot iron doors and Nepomuk quickly released the bread into the oven before dropping the paddle and tending to her. But in these few seconds, Enya's burns had already begun to heal and were barely visible anymore.

"I'm so sorry; that's why I always had a thick oven mitt hanging right here." He pointed at a hook on the side of the oven. "The hook is there, I just forgot to make the mitt."

"It's alright, I've suffered worse," Enya responded as she bent her completely healed fingers.

"You know, I'm here if you need to talk," offered Nepomuk, who was becoming a little curious about what this young woman could have suffered in her short life.

"What's next?" she asked instead.

"Now, we wait again. But it shouldn't take too long."

After about twenty minutes, Nepomuk judged by the sweet smell emanating from the oven that the bread was ready. Like a reflex, he wanted to grab his oven mitt but only grasped thin air. For a moment he considered opening the oven door with his bare hands, but even though wounds seemed to heal quickly in this place, he wanted to avoid the pain.

So, he drew the rough outline of a mitt on the ground and, moments later, an equally rough and frayed cloth mitt lay where previously there had been nothing.

He picked it up and had to double it over; it was poorly made, but it was good enough to open the door unharmed. A moment later, he had shimmied the bread back onto the paddle and pulled out a perfectly formed and golden loaf.

He and Enya bent over the steaming bread and soaked in its hot and sweet steamy aroma.

They sat back down facing the river and Nepomuk broke the bread in half. He felt as alive as he could do, considering that he was dead. It was so nice to have someone to share this place with that he now understood Humphrey's eagerness to keep him by his side.

They sat quietly and enjoyed the bread. Although neither of them felt hungry, the fresh bread with its sweet pieces of fruit created a long-missed ecstasy in his mouth.

"Can we make some more bread?" asked Enya, still chewing on her last bite.

"Sure. What's your favourite?"

Enya shrugged. "We never had much bread. A friend, or at least I thought that's what he was, gave me a piece once that had little brown seeds in it. It tasted strange, like a story from far away."

"Do you mean sesame?"

"I don't think so."

"I think I know what you mean. Caraway seeds. Love your description of it. It's most commonly made with sourdough and rye flour."

"Can you make that?"

"Can I? Of course I can: I'm a master baker and I was a pretty good confectioner, too. First, though, we should prepare our workspace. Making bread on the floor is neither good for the bread nor for your back."

Nepomuk measured the space around the oven – not that there was anything in his way, at least not yet.

"A good bakery or kitchen is constructed in a triangle. In one corner is the oven, in another your workstation, and in the third your pantry with a sink. Everything should be about three steps away from each other so that you have enough space to turn and move around but can also reach everything with minimal effort."

He drew rough squares in the sand where everything had to go.

"Okay, how about you start on the storage area? Build some shelves and a sink, and I'll make the work area with bowls and utensils?" suggested Nepomuk.

"I've never built anything, definitely not a sink."

"But you have seen one and know how it's supposed to look?"

"I guess."

"Just give it a go."

They went on to refine the drawings on the ground. Several people walked by and looked interested but none of them stopped for long. When Nepomuk turned to see how Enya was doing, she was pretend-hammering some invisible boards together. Nepomuk had to laugh at her mime.

"What?" she asked, sulking.

"Maybe use some screws as well. We don't want it to fall apart when we place the bowls and flour on it. And make sure the boards are deep enough."

Enya pushed her hammer into her imaginary utensil belt and pulled out a screwdriver, taking on the posture of a seasoned builder.

Nepomuk bent back down to draw a few circles into the ground that would become their mixing bowls, but only a second later he looked back up when Enya exclaimed in surprise.

She stood in front of a fully formed shelf. Yes, it was a little rickety and some screws needed tightening. The panels were quite uneven, with remnants of bark, and it looked as though she had felled the tree and cut the boards herself. But it was workable. The sink, though, which she made later, did not work, possibly because it was not connected to a water source. But even if they laid a pipe to the river, the spout looked like a solid metal snake and the handles didn't turn.

Nepomuk's creations were only slightly better, at least when it came to the metal bowls and the bucket that he had made to fetch water from the river. Everything appeared as though it was as good as the knowledge that the creator had about making the item, all the way down to sourcing the material.

In the end though, they had enough to work with, and a big balloon of satisfaction swelled in Nepomuk's chest. Enya's youthful appearance had returned. Her eyes were still big like an innocent child but filled with the grief of an entire lifetime.

"It looks pretty crap," she said, a smile curling around her lips.

"Are you kidding? This is amazing. We made something out of nothing."

"How do you think this works? I mean, is this magic?"

"I'm not sure. Something like it. I think the more you know about the thing you are trying to make the better it gets."

"I guess I don't know how to make a sink."

"Maybe we'll find a plumber to fix it."

"That would be wise. I don't know much about anything, I'm afraid."

"I can teach you how to make bread if you like."

She looked at him as if she was about to start crying again. "I'd like that."

"Okay, let's get started. We need some water." He passed the wonky bucket to her. "I'm afraid I don't know how to work metal very well either."

"It looks good; very artisanal."

"It does, doesn't it?"

They smiled at each other, and Enya went off to fetch some water while Nepomuk filled two large bowls with sand and several smaller bowls with dust, fine gravel, and larger rocks.

When she came back, Nepomuk introduced her to the science of bread making.

"There are two different types of bread dough: one uses yeast, the other lactic acid bacteria."

Enya seemed disgusted.

"Lactic acid bacteria are really good for your gut."

"If you say so."

"The yeast produces carbon dioxide, which leavens the dough, and the bacteria give the sourdough its typical flavour. One of the best, if you ask me."

"It sounds like chemical warfare, if you ask me."

Nepomuk laughed out loud. "Maybe. Let's try it, though, before making any judgements. Here, for your caraway bread, we make a yeast dough with two thirds rye and one third wheat flour."

Nepomuk gave her the two bowls that contained, to his satisfaction, perfectly sieved rye and wheat flour, just as he remembered.

"What's rye and what's the difference?" asked Enya sceptically.

"Rye and wheat are both grasses that were cultivated to yield larger grains." Nepomuk paused at Enya's bored look. "In short, rye flour makes for denser and more aromatic dough, perfect for caraway seeds, and wheat flour makes for fluffier and often sweeter-tasting doughs. For this bread, we mix them to get the best of both. Here, measure two cups of rye and one cup of wheat. I'll be right back."

He filled a metal bowl with water and placed it on top of the oven to warm its contents.

"And now?" asked Enya.

"We add all the dry ingredients first. A pinch of salt and a small handful of yeast." He placed two smaller bowls in front of her that now contained the required ingredients. "I forgot to make more measuring cups, but this will do for now. Give it a good stir."

Nepomuk got the bowl from above the oven and poured the warm liquid into the bowl with the other ingredients while Enya was mixing it with her hands.

"This is buttermilk, my secret ingredient. It brings out the tangy flavour of the rye. And finally, we add some ground and whole caraway seeds. Keep kneading the dough until it is one smooth ball."

Enya did as she was told. "Puh, this is a whole-body workout."

"Keep going, it's looking good. See how it stops sticking to the sides? Alright, now we let the yeast do its thing, which it does best when it's warm and undisturbed."

Nepomuk placed his handkerchief over the bowl and moved it closer to the oven.

"The dough needs to double in size. Until then, we are going to make a Herman."

"A what?" Enya looked perplexed.

"A Herman. It's something I used to do with my kids."

"Who is Herman?"

"It's a sourdough that you can give to your friends. If you keep feeding it, you will always have some dough ready to make bread or cake or anything you fancy. It's also good if you don't have any yeast or soda at hand. Just add a little bit of Herman to your baking project."

"Sounds like the dream of every little girl."

Nepomuk talked Enya through the different ingredients, which she mixed in a jar instead of a bowl. "Herman has a sweet tooth and needs a little bit of sugar to feel well. And to give him a little bit of a head start, we add some lactic acid bacteria."

Herman turned out quite a bit moister than the yeast dough they made before. Instead of kneading it with her hands, Nepomuk gave Enya a wooden spoon to stir everything together.

"And now we let Herman grow up. It's your responsibility to look after him. He needs to be stirred every day, and every fifth day, you need to feed him with some more flour, sugar and milk."

"I should tell you; I was never great with pets."

"You'll be fine. I'll remind you and eating a bit of Herman every now and then should give you the right motivation."

"I think I'm gonna be sick."

"You'll see," laughed Nepomuk as he left to check on the yeast dough.

The dough had risen exactly as Nepomuk had predicted and now Enya got to form her first ever bread loaf. Nepomuk scored the surface several times before Enya sprinkled more caraway seeds on top.

This time, the smell of the baking bread and their little bakery, which despite its rickety appearance stood out magnificently in this desolation, attracted several deceased.

"This reminds me of my childhood," said a young boy who had been an old man several steps earlier. "How much longer until it is ready?"

As soon as the bread was out of the oven and had at least some chance to cool down, a line of people was waiting, hoping to get some provisions for their journey.

"The first slice goes to my apprentice. She came up with the idea." Nepomuk cut a piece off and presented it to Enya.

"Thank you," whispered Enya, deeply inhaling the earthy aroma. "For you," she finally said and passed her piece to the little boy. And with this, they gave away every bit of their caraway bread. When it was gone, Enya started on the next batch right away.

"It is nice to have something to give that you don't mind giving away," she said as she worked the dough. "Oh look!" she exclaimed when she put the covered bowl down near the oven. "Herman is breathing."

Herman the sourdough had started to throw his first bubbles, and they watched as he came alive.

"That is what my daughter said when we made it the first time," said Nepomuk.

"My mom never did anything with me. Certainly nothing this exciting."

"Why not?"

"I don't know. She was always too busy, if you can call smoking and scrolling through your phone being busy."

"Then what did you do all day?" asked Nepomuk.

"Smoking and scrolling through my phone," she said dolefully. "Once, I tried to grow sunflowers. I picked the seeds off some stale bread. Didn't work."

Nepomuk watched her. As her appearance changed back to show the sorrows that she had suffered, he felt deeply saddened. He had always strived to make the most of his life as he knew that it was his only chance. To think that some people were so lost or maybe kicked to the ground one too many times to be able to have at least some enjoyable moments, no matter how short their life was, was heart-breaking.

"Do you never sleep in this place?" asked Enya, as if she could not bear thinking about her life anymore.

"You don't have to, but just like eating, you can do it if you please."

"I think it would please me very much right now."

"Just lie down and imagine that you're in a soft featherbed," recommended Nepomuk.

"That easy, huh?"

"That easy."

 Chapter 6

Enya curled up with her back to the oven and fell asleep.

Nepomuk, however, was restless. He cleaned up their kitchen and then began making another batch of dough. At first, he just let instinct take over and carried out all the steps of measuring, mixing, and kneading as if in a trance. But when he found that the sand in the small bowls had turned into cardamom and cinnamon, and the gravel into redcurrants, he knew he was making Blanka's favourite bread.

He made a baker's dozen loaves, and as soon as the bread was out of the oven, the deceased waited in line again to get a small piece. It was funny how something you didn't really need could still be so desired. But he saw the smiles on people's faces as they smelled or nibbled on his baked goods and knew that it was simply a comforting thing to eat warm bread, especially after a traumatic experience like dying. He should make some croissants next. Maybe they could offer hot chocolate with it.

Remembering how Luella always liked to dip her croissants into the sweet drink when she came back from her exchange year in France, he gave away the last piece of bread.

"Sorry, folks, all out for today!" he called, and the crowd dissipated, but not without some grumbling and a few snide remarks.

How could people in the afterlife still be so demanding if there was nothing they truly needed? If they really wanted it, they could just imagine it for themselves. And then he thought he should have kept one piece of bread for Blanka and felt painfully reminded about how much she liked it. Next time, he resolved, he would hold one bread roll back, just for her, just in case.

People kept stopping to ask if he had any bread left and Nepomuk grew tired answering that they would be open again the next day, which was technically not possible as there was no time. He made a sign that read 'open' on one side and 'closed' on the other and hung it from his workbench.

When things fell a little quieter, he lost himself in his memories again. He remembered how they bought that house that had their little shop out front, the bakery in the back and their living quarters on top. The children had chosen the rather garish combination of pink and turquoise to paint the front, but that had also meant that they were visible to everyone from either corner of the street and beyond.

He had always hoped that Marek would take on the family business and had made the poor boy help in the bakery in his spare time, but Marek's interests were more on the business side of things. For a while, he happily kneaded or rather punched the dough, helped his father take in deliveries or ran around the neighbourhood to put advertisements into letterboxes. But he soon became careless as his thoughts started to wander to other interests. Nepomuk found leaflets dumped in bins and had to spend an entire Monday morning cleaning up the bakery after Marek had accidentally dropped a whole sack of flour from the overhead storage onto the floor before he was ready to catch it. Everything looked like a beautiful wintry landscape, including a life-size snowman.

In the end, Marek's more analytical interests were useful for a while to keep their books in order, but without anyone who would provide the goods to sell in their shop there wasn't much hope of keeping the bakery afloat beyond his and Blanka's retirement.

When they came to retire, they sold the bakery to someone who made it into a patisserie café. Nepomuk was glad that it hadn't been turned into an electronic haven or boarded up entirely. Luella became one of the patisserie's best customers for as long as she was still living at home, and they made sure that they always had a croissant put aside just for her.

Nepomuk lay down and closed his eyes as he let his mind wander. Where were his family now? Maybe he had grandkids by now? He could hear some children laughing as they always did when they found something amusing, like pretending the floor was lava or hearing a funny name like Mister Longbottom.

He opened his eyes again and kept hearing children talking to each other.

"And how did you die?" asked the voice of a little girl.

"Oh, I was running super-fast, you know, like Sonic, and then I just fell into a hole. It was really dark, and I hit my head," said the voice of a little boy.

As it happened, when Nepomuk sat up, he saw the two children cowering at the side of his bakery. Curious what they were doing, he walked over and saw that they were watering some tiny two-leafed plants that had just emerged from the ground.

"Look!" exclaimed the girl when she noticed him. "I planted sunflowers."

"Enya?" Nepomuk asked, surprised.

"Yes, oh, and this is Danilo. Danilo, this is Nepomuk. He makes really nice bread."

"Hi," said Danilo, with a grin. "Is this yours?" He pointed at his bakery set-up.

"Yes. Shall we make some bread?"

"Nah."

"Oh, why not?"

"Because I don't want to." And with that Danilo whizzed to the river and back. "Did you see how fast I was?"

"Yes."

"My dad says I'm gonna be the fastest person in the world when I grow up. But I'm already faster than a car. Do you wanna count?"

"Okay?"

And off he went again to the river and back. Nepomuk admitted that the boy was as fast as a car, even though he probably didn't realize it himself.

"How much?" Danilo asked when he came back once more.

"Fifteen," answered Nepomuk.

"That's super-fast," exclaimed Danilo, excited, and sped off again.

Nepomuk felt dizzy just watching this bundle of energy, who had now started to throw stones into the river.

A little melody drew his attention back to Enya, who was sitting next to her sunflowers.

"That's very nice," he said and sat next to her.

"My nan used to sing it to me. She died when I was seven."

"Was that when you tried to grow sunflowers last time?"

Enya nodded. She reminded him so much of his own daughter right now, and Danilo was exactly like his son at this age.

"Did you see that?" shouted Danilo from the river. "I made it jump like six trillion times." The boy picked up another stone and flicked it across the river.

"I always wanted to do that too," said Enya excitedly and ran off to the shoreline.

"Hey, is this shack ever open?" asked a man in a business suit next to Nepomuk. "I don't have all day."

"We don't have anything in storage at the moment, but I could make a fresh batch now," said Nepomuk in a friendly tone.

"Alright. Is there anywhere I could get a coffee while I wait?"

Nepomuk looked at the customer a little too long, but his questions just seemed to be too ridiculous, considering that there was plainly nothing else around them.

"What?" asked the man.

"You could just make yourself a cup and get some water from the river," suggested Nepomuk.

"Make a cup? Do I look like I know how to make cups?"

He looked as though he didn't know how to make any-thing. Nepomuk scratched the shape of a cup into the ground and a second later handed a wonky pottery mug to the man.

"How did you do that?" asked the man suspiciously.

"I just imagined it," explained Nepomuk.

"And the coffee?"

"As I said, just fetch some water from the river, or fill it with sand, whatever suits you best."

The man looked at him as if he were stupid or at the very least tried to hold him for a fool.

"Enya, do you want to help me again?" Nepomuk called out as he turned to his workbench.

"Later," came back the response from the river.

To his dismay, he found that his kitchen had fallen into some disarray and not even his imagination could fix it. Instead, he had to create some tools and screws to repair the wobbly countertop, as well as some mortar to fix some loose stones in the oven.

He was still repairing things when he saw the yuppie walking back from the river, taking a sip from his cup and spluttering it back out again.

He could hear him cursing and complaining all the way.

"This is the worst coffee I have ever tasted!"

"Have you ever made coffee yourself?" asked Nepomuk.

"Course not."

"Lucky that you don't need coffee here."

"Well, that's not up to you. Is the food ready?"

"No, sir. Making bread takes time."

"It shouldn't take that long. How do you even stay in business?"

"Well, I'm not here to make money. I just enjoy making bread."

The businessman grunted and eyed Nepomuk from top to bottom. "With that attitude you'll never win in life."

"Lucky this purgatory, or whatever this place is, is not about winning anymore, and I doubt that life was about that either," said Nepomuk.

"Whether this is some sort of punishment or last chance, you'd better get some business advice. I've seen many small shops like yours making bad decisions when all they needed was someone like me to come in and whip it into shape."

"I think I'm good. As I said, I just like making bread. Sharing it with others is just a pleasant side effect that I can afford here."

"Not a good way to bail yourself out of purgatory, if you ask me."

Nepomuk had heard enough. This man wasn't right, certainly not right for him. He picked up the bread paddle and drew several lines around his workstation, elaborating here and there and finally scraping a long line between the man and his workbench.

The man watched him with a derisive smile. He took another sip from his cup but spat it out again.

When Nepomuk was finished he positioned himself right in front of the man with the line dividing them. He smiled with superiority, which seemed to annoy his opposite tremendously. In his vision, he saw his old bakery in pink and turquoise, the counter from which Blanka had sold his baked creations, and even two small bedrooms near the oven. When he had walked through the rooms in his mind and found everything to his satisfaction, the walls and windows, doors and roof appeared all around him. He stood in his open shop door and with one last smile he closed the door on the man.

"This will have repercussions," exclaimed the man and stomped away.

Nepomuk turned around and took a deep breath. Everything looked exactly like it had been. Remembering everything started to have its advantages, but he also added little improvements here and there that he had always wanted to make. The large front window now had beautiful stained glass inserts depicting harvest scenes. The shelves behind the counter had rustic corn carvings and instead of the shelf on wheels that had functioned as their door behind the counter, he had imagined a swinging saloon door. The missing display area was replaced by an extended counter without the need for a till, as he wouldn't be taking money anymore. It felt good to be able to provide food without needing to worry about his own livelihood. This was how rich people must feel.

Nepomuk had started the dough for Sunday rolls — without days he might as well make them all the time — when the little bell above the door rang. For a second, he worried that it was that wretched businessman again, but the shuffling of little feet told him otherwise.

"What did you do?" asked Enya when she stormed into the bakehouse followed by Danilo.

"I made some upgrades to our shop. Do you like it?"

"It looks amazing. What are you making?"

"I thought I'd make some Sunday rolls."

"Can we help you?"

"Sure, but check on Herman first. I think he needs a stir."

"Who's Herman?" asked Danilo.

"Come, I'll show you."

Nepomuk began kneading the dough. As he was making enough to fill a shelf in the shop, he was using the workbench instead of a bowl. It felt good to do manual labour and the giggling of the children filled his heart with happiness. If only he would step out into the shop and find Blanka to share this existence with him once more.

"Do you wanna hear a joke?" he heard Danilo ask.

"Go on," Enya replied.

"What did the roll say to his sad friend?"

"I don't know."

"Tomorrow will be butter." Danilo cracked up laughing at his own joke and when they came back to Nepomuk he was told the same joke again.

The kids helped splendidly, although Nepomuk had to re-roll everything, as their little hands were not yet strong enough to form smooth balls. With some leftover dough, Nepomuk formed bread into the shapes of men with raisins as eyes and coarse sugar clumps as decoration, which Danilo found very exciting.

He couldn't wait to play with the baked men and burned his fingers when he tried to grab them straight from the oven paddle.

"Wait!" called Nepomuk in vain and one of the breadmen landed on the ground with a broken leg.

"Ow," moaned Danilo, almost more about the broken breadman than his burned fingers, probably because the burn was healed almost as soon as he had picked up the breadman from the floor.

"If you must handle hot bread, you balance it on your fingertips and then you move them, as if you are drumming from underneath. That way, neither finger touches the bread for so long that it can burn."

Nepomuk showed them how to do it. Here it only prevented the short sensation of getting burned, but why suffer even for a second if you could avoid it?

"Can we play with them?" asked Danilo, who had grown restless watching Nepomuk place the rolls on cooling racks.

"Sure. Take them all and see if there are any other kids outside who would like one."

"Cool!" shouted Danilo as he picked up two to walk them to the door. "Hey, you wanna race?" he made one breadman ask the other. "You're toast," the other breadman answered, and with that Danilo raced out of the shop, the doorbell ringing furiously.

Enya grabbed an arm full of breadmen and rolls but turned around in the door and smirked. "I think baking is a labour of loaf."

"What can I say, I'm on a roll," answered Nepomuk, and he didn't think his heart could take any more happiness, considering the circumstances.

In his head he was already planning all the varieties of breads and rolls he was going to make next. Maybe he would even make some cakes and create a display cabinet for them. Through the window he saw Enya passing a breadman to another eight-year-old girl, but the next time he looked up, she was back to her twenty-two-year-old self and looked frozen in time.

Curious and a little uneasy, Nepomuk stepped outside to see what Enya was looking at that made her change again so drastically.

A few steps down the bank, another shop had opened. It was a café that looked rather windswept, and the businessman was berating the woman who had apparently created the shop.

"I don't know anything about building a house; I know how to make coffee!" she shouted.

"Let's hope that's true. I won't think twice about dismissing you if the turnover is not good or I hear any complaints," said the businessman and then gestured for the barista to go inside and start her job.

"You know what? You don't own me. Go fuck yourself."

The woman turned and walked straight into the open desert without another look.

The businessman raised his arms in disbelief. "You know, if I had given up that easily when my boss pushed me a little, I would have jumped from that building a lot sooner! No, I had lost hundreds of millions of dollars before I bowed out!"

What an outlandish thing to say, thought Nepomuk. Did that man really think it was a badge of honour to kill himself after he had made a mistake that sounded as if it had cost many people dearly.

The woman just flipped him off and walked on. The businessman turned his attention to another young woman who had just arrived and was looking curiously at the crooked café.

"Are you okay?" asked Nepomuk, watching the scene from the distance.

"No," said Enya.

"I think it's a rather nice idea to have a café next to our bakery."

"It's not that. It's him."

Enya stared with horrified eyes at the businessman who was walking towards them. Her face seemed to dissolve back to a teenager, and there were clearly some memories that made her unable to move.

"Now, have you finished baking?" the man asked, glancing at Enya.

Nepomuk knew that he had recognized her as well.

Chapter 7

"I HAVE SOME ROLLS ready, if you'd like one," Nepomuk suggested.

"How about a BLT?" asked the obnoxious businessman in return.

"I'm sorry; only rolls. But maybe you can convince someone to open a butcher and grow some vegetables next."

"Fine, but I don't have any money."

"That's alright. I told you I'm just happy to do a good deed."

"I'm sure you are," grinned the man and followed Nepomuk into the shop. He grabbed his roll before strolling back to the café. "Still, let me know if you need any business advice."

Nepomuk was glad the man had left. He resolved to never request anything from him because there would always be an ulterior motive; surely not the right way to go about purgatory.

Nepomuk found Enya crouching around the corner behind her sunflowers, which had already grown a metre and were showing their first buds.

"Do you want to tell me who he is?" asked Nepomuk as he sat down next to her.

"His name is Knight Lukas. I met him when I was fifteen. He must have been like twenty-five then. I don't know. I was out dancing, drinking. He paid for some of my drinks and then offered to drive me home." Enya's voice began to crack.

Nepomuk could imagine what happened next and disgust swelled his throat. But even more, he felt his heart break for Enya. All he could do, and wanted to do, was to take her into his arms and protect her.

"I know I wasn't a child of innocence. I started smoking weed when I was ten, and took ecstasy on most nights out," Enya cried.

"That is no excuse for anyone to take advantage of you."

"My nan had always told me to stay away from drugs. My dad was an alcoholic. Walked in front of a lorry when I was three. My mother was an alcoholic. There was no one to stop me from anything. Least of all me."

"Why are you hiding here?" interrupted Danilo suddenly.

"We are not hiding. We were just looking after Enya's sunflowers. They, like us, need some love to grow up strong," Nepomuk answered.

"Hmm. Why is she crying?" Danilo asked.

"Enya is a little sad about her life," Nepomuk tried to explain.

"Why?"

"Because ..." Nepomuk was lost for words.

"Because I didn't have any sunflowers," helped out Enya as she wiped away her tears and cracked a smile.

"You look old," said Danilo when he saw her face.

"Thanks," Enya laughed through her tears.

"Hey, wanna hear a joke?"

"Go on."

"What's brown and sticky?"

"Poo?"

"No, a stick," Danilo crowed. "What did the policeman say to his belly button?"

"I don't know."

"You're under a vest."

Danilo burst into laughter at his own jokes again and Nepomuk and Enya couldn't help but joined in, not so much because they thought the jokes were funny but because the child's laughter was so infectious.

"You are like a fountain of jokes," said Nepomuk.

"Do you wanna hear another one? A knight told it to me."

"Who?"

"That man there." Danilo pointed at the businessman, who was talking to someone by the river and gesturing wildly into the distance. "He's a real knight, you know."

"Stay away from him," croaked Enya.

"Why?"

"Because he's a bad man."

"Why?"

"He hurt me very much."

Danilo looked torn. "Then I will protect you," he said heroically, and his features changed slightly to have a more prominent jawline and darker slicked-back hair. Nepomuk had also not noticed before that the boy was wearing his red underpants over his trousers.

"Come on, how about we make some Christmas cookies?" suggested Nepomuk to break the silence.

"Oh, yes. Can we make a gingerbread house with sugar windows and a chimney?" asked Danilo enthusiastically.

"Of course we can."

Nepomuk offered Enya a hand and, with Danilo walking ahead as their bodyguard, they rounded the corner and went back into the bakery. The child was looking odder and odder, somehow like a misshapen cartoon of a superhero in a little boy's body.

Even though Nepomuk kept them going until all the shelves in the shop were filled and Herman was stirred and well fed, Enya did not change back into the little girl, but remained the haunted teenager.

Danilo got absorbed in making his gingerbread house on the round table in the shop. It quickly expanded to include a slide from the rooftop that landed in a marshmallow swimming pool, a trampoline made from melted gummy bears, a choo-choo train that balanced on the edge of the table and had candyfloss steaming out of its chimney, and finally a loop-de-loop that twisted all around the table and back up again. He was so immersed in his building adventure that he didn't notice the stream of customers who came in and out, watching him with curiosity. Nepomuk only asked him whether he could continue his expansion outside, which he gladly did, when he started to get in the way of other people by spanning a gingerbread cable cart across the room and along the window to connect his alpine toboggan run.

As dying never ceased, so continued the influx of customers who wanted to get bread for their way onward, and Nepomuk found that even with Enya working unremittingly, they could not keep the shelves full and had to close to restock.

"Do you want to lie down for a while?" asked Nepomuk, as Enya hung the now threadbare oven mitt back on its hook. She looked tired, although her gloom had lifted slightly.

"Nah, I think I'll keep going. I had an idea for a yeast bread with nuts, but instead of mixing the nuts in, you could roll it up and have a nice ring pattern, when you cut it. Like a tree or something."

"That sounds very good. You are on your way to becoming a master baker yourself."

"I wish I had met you when I was alive."

"I would have taken you on as an apprentice."

"I doubt that."

"How about a coffee?"

Enya nodded and Nepomuk left, curious to see how the café next door was coming along and dealing with the never-ending customers.

He stood rooted to the ground as soon as he stepped outside. There wasn't just a café; there was also a bubble tea shop, a Wild West saloon where Danilo was running in circles pretending to duel with another little boy, a massage parlour, a sushi bar, and a bed-and-breakfast complete with a white picket fence, veranda, and wooden shutters. But the most extraordinary thing was the hill that was now softly sweeping up about three hundred metres behind this newly established waterfront and the white marble mansion that overlooked it all.

Nepomuk wandered in amazement over to the café and waited in line.

"I wish there were more choices. It isn't really Paradise if you have to wait for hours to get a coffee," someone said in front of Nepomuk.

"Yeah, what's the point of being dead if this is what you get," said another person.

"Well, you don't really have a choice, do you?" said Nepomuk, aghast.

"What do you know?"

"Nothing really, but I don't think anyone was supposed to stay here for very long."

"That's not our fault, is it? We just wanted to grab a quick coffee and be off again. There isn't much worth staying for anyways."

The queue moved on and Nepomuk could see a poor woman rotating like a little engine to keep the coffee machine running and filling mug after mug after mug.

"Finally. You should really do that name-calling thing to keep up, like they do at Starbucks," the person in front of Nepomuk lectured the barista.

"I'm sorry, but without another person to make the coffees or take the orders, I cannot work any faster," the woman said tentatively.

"Right, well. I'll take a large latte macchiato. Do you have anything to eat?"

"I'm sorry, I can only do espressos or americanos."

"Are you serious?"

"I'm very sorry."

"An americano with milk then."

"Sorry, we don't have any milk."

"What is this place? Hell?"

"Please, if you don't want to order anything, move along."

Nepomuk could see how the barista struggled to stay polite and sane.

"You know, you could simply close the shop and take a break. It's not like people here can't make their own coffee," suggested Nepomuk.

"Could you please wait until it's your turn? We have all been waiting in line," the person rebuked Nepomuk. "One Americano and a muffin to go."

The barista filled a paper cup and handed it over. "We don't sell any food, but maybe the bakery next door has something to your liking."

"Outrageous."

"I can guarantee you that the bakery has nothing you would want," said Nepomuk.

"And how would you know?"

"Because I'm the baker and I do not wish to see you in my shop."

"Well, you've definitely lost my business."

"Glad to be of service."

With that, the person finally waltzed away.

"You should really just close shop and enjoy yourself for a while," suggested Nepomuk.

"I can't, I'm already behind," said the barista quietly.

"How can you be behind when there is nothing that you need to achieve?" asked Nepomuk.

"Look, the only thing I know is how to make coffee and having this little café to pay my debts is the best that could have happened to me to pass my purgatory."

"Your purgatory? Who told you that you're in purgatory?" Nepomuk had a dreadful suspicion.

"The owner of these shops."

"Knight Lukas?"

"Yes, he owns all the shops here. Well, I guess apart from your bakery."

"He owns all the ...?" Nepomuk was flabbergasted. "So, open your own café, or anything you like. This is the afterlife; you don't owe anyone anything."

"I can't open my own café, there is no other."

"Just make it yourself."

"Make it?"

"Yes, you can make anything you want here. Look." Nepomuk moved his hands as if he were sculpting a clay cup.

As he was smoothing his hands upwards, a large mug appeared out of thin air.

"How did you do that?" the barista gasped.

"Just like everyone is making things here. Just like you have your coffee grounds and water in your machine. You just imagine it: the more you know about how the thing has to be made, the better it is."

"Oi, move along!" someone shouted from further back.

"Shut up!" said the person behind Nepomuk, who had witnessed the creation of the mug. "Are you saying we can do whatever we want?"

"As far as I can tell, yes."

"So, I could go and make myself a Mercedes Benz?"

"Yes, but I reckon you'd need to know something about car mechanics to make it work properly."

"Lucky, I had my own garage," said the man and turned around to go outside.

Several people, including Nepomuk and the barista, followed, to the annoyance of the people further in the back who had not seen or heard the conversation.

Outside, the mechanic stood rather helpless. "How do I start?"

"You can draw into the sand or pretend you are building a car. That worked for me," said Nepomuk.

He held his breath, just like everyone else who had crowded around them. He hoped it would work so he wouldn't be seen as a fraud.

"Alright. Give me some space," said the mechanic and gestured to leave a larger circle around him.

He began by drawing a rough outline on the ground and then moved on, pretending that he was screwing wheels in place, bending and polishing the chassis all around, opening the hood to install an engine, and when he closed the hood again with a bang, a black Mercedes Roadster stood there, sparkling in the desert.

A murmur of amazement went through the crowd and then laughter as the man tried to open the car but found it locked.

"You need to make a key!" shouted someone.

The mechanic tapped his head in thanks for the suggestion and then drew a small shape into the ground, picked up the key, jumped into the driver's seat and revved the engine.

The crowed parted with whistles and shouts of admiration, and off sped the car mechanic into the distance.

As soon as he was gone, another man jumped into the circle and copied the same steps the mechanic had done. He drew a square into the ground, hammered and polished the air, opened the hood to fix an engine, and when he banged the hood shut again, his car appeared racing red, but with wheels that weren't perfectly round, a windshield that didn't fit the frame properly, and a chassis that resembled that of a Porsche but seemed to have been melted together with a 1986 Ford Taurus.

The people jeered as he opened the car only to have the door fall to his feet. He nonetheless sat in and drove off with an engine that sounded clogged and ticked like a time bomb. Unsurprisingly, he only made it fifty metres before the hood blew open and released a cloud of black smoke.

In no time, hundreds of people were making cars all around. Most had a similar fate to the Porsche Taurus, but some BMWs, Rolls Royces and Lamborghinis worked smoothly or even looked like works of art with extravagantly swung heck spoilers or newly invented car logos. Some people even made horse carriages, but no one managed to make the required horses, so they just stood on the bank of the river and quickly fell into disrepair again.

Nepomuk pushed his way through the ever-extending crowd and watched the things everyone was making, from ballgowns to beer cans, diamond rings to dolls. Someone even attempted to create a yacht on the river, but it sank unceremoniously and was quickly swept away.

Most things, just like Nepomuk's mug, oven or bakery, looked too small for their purpose or somewhat deformed, and you could quickly tell where the expertise of the creator lay.

The whole area soon looked like a maze of a market surrounded by a waste yard, and what had seemed to be innocent fun turned into a nightmarish struggle to even put one foot in front of the other.

As Nepomuk tried to find his bakery again, market stands and shops popped up everywhere, most offering the discarded mishaps where people had tried to create something beyond their skills, interspersed with more and more coffee shops, as if coffee was the lifeblood of the dead. At least the junkshops meant that some cleaning up happened.

Nepomuk felt that this was a horrible place, and he still couldn't quite perceive how it had ballooned so quickly. After a small eternity, he finally saw some pink and turquoise blink through the mayhem and found that a pick 'n' mix sweet stand had opened right in front of his door next to a cheese and wine bar, a barber, and another coffee shop behind.

He closed the door behind him and drew a deep breath before lowering the blinds to shut out the tumult in front of his window. It was pleasantly quiet inside, although Danilo's gingerbread amusement park had crumbled down and had left heaps of sand and gravel on the floor.

Enya looked out of the kitchen, her face and clothes dusted in flour.

"What is happening out there?"

"I'm afraid I have unleashed hell."

They peeked through the blinds at the shoppers, who had started to barter loudly to get a desired object or food item or beverage.

Chapter 8

THE SETTLEMENT THAT HAD started with an oven to make bread had grown like a cancerous ulcer from people's dreams and desires fuelled by the thousands of newly departed that arrived at every waking hour.

Before, without anything welcoming them on this side of the river, everyone had sooner or later just moved on in the hopes of finding something more hospitable than dust and gravel. But now that people had found out that anyone could create whatever they fancied, more often than not after a fashion, there seemed to be no reason to move on. After all, what more could you wish for than a land of plenty with no rules or regulations where neither thirst nor hunger, poverty nor illness existed? Even death was off the cards.

Nepomuk and Enya watched the hustle and bustle outside their bakery through the blinds with worry.

"Where is Danilo?" asked Enya.

"I don't know."

The last time Nepomuk had seen the boy was in a pistol duel in front of the saloon a few houses down. Carefully, Nepomuk cracked the door open, and Enya followed him outside. The noises were deafening. People shouted out their latest offers, bartered even louder, cars backfired in the distance, and worryingly, the crunching and crushing of wood and stone indicated that many shops and stalls could collapse at any time.

As Nepomuk and Enya wriggled through the hurly-burly, they saw that some market stands were already crumbling to bits. Under their feet, shards of pottery, games consoles, and even bits of metal were pounded back into the dust they were made from.

"Danilo!" Nepomuk shouted.

They hit the shore of the river, which was the only piece of the original landscape that seemed to have been left untouched, at least since the sinking of the yacht.

Nepomuk thought about whether it was his responsibility to look out for the boy, considering that nothing could really harm him anymore, when they turned back and bent their necks in amazement.

He thought he had seen everything, but the monstrosity that rose high up into the sky behind his bakery was unbelievable, and he immediately knew where to find Danilo.

With dozens of loops and turns and neck-breaking falls stretched a rollercoaster with its tracks around the buildings, as there was not just the white marble mansion but a whole town now sprawling over the plain. In between the rollercoaster tracks other amusement rides had been installed: water slides, foam slides, slides with rainbow-coloured slime, toboggan runs with real snow falling airily on the slope. The pièce de resistance, however, was a life-size bouncy castle with a moat filled with balls. This creation obviously came and unashamedly from the boundless imagination of a child.

Screaming joyfully with seemingly the rest of the perished children as well as several young-at-heart elderly deceased, Danilo sat in a rollercoaster cart speeding above the crowds.

"What do we do now?" asked Enya.

"I don't know. He seems to know what he is doing, so let's go back inside. This ruckus makes it difficult to think."

"There needs to be someone to bring order to this mayhem," said Enya when they were back in the safety of the bakery.

Surprisingly, the closed sign seemed to make their little shop in a way invisible to people, or maybe there was such a plethora of everything out there that nobody required yet another shop to be open to fulfil their desires.

In a way Nepomuk was saddened that nobody came in anymore talking about their memories of long-gone childhoods. Suddenly he even felt anxious that with all the ruckus outside he would now most definitely miss Blanka. She would avoid this place and never even think about him running a bakery in the middle of this circus.

"You are right; this can't continue," Nepomuk said decisively.

But what could he do? There were no rules to obey, no laws that were broken, no authority to complain to.

His mind felt muffled when the door was flung open, and several people pushed in apparently fleeing from a brawl that had broken out at the wine and cheese bar.

"What a horrible place this is," said a woman in her late sixties with a well-put-together appearance.

"I died so peacefully surrounded by my loved ones and this is what I have to put up with?" questioned an ancient-looking man with a tear-streaked face.

"I didn't think hell existed," said a third.

"It's human nature, unleashed," answered Nepomuk, and all eyes turned to him.

"This is not human nature, these are animals," said the put-together woman, enraged.

"Unleashed, as he said," whispered Enya.

"Someone needs to do something about it," argued the woman.

"Why am I here?" whimpered the old man.

"I'm not sure this was supposed to happen, but I'm afraid we can't stop it," said Nepomuk.

"Of course we can. It only needs someone with authority and a little imagination," spat the woman.

"Imagination is what got us into this mess," argued Nepomuk.

"Oh, and you are an expert on this?" questioned the woman.

Why was everybody so argumentative today, wondered Nepomuk. But then, he might have been more demanding himself if he had found this hypercharged Las Vegas that promised everybody everything, instead of a solitary wasteland.

"I don't know how this afterlife works, but it appears that you can create everything out of nothing as long as you have enough knowledge about how that thing would have been made back in the living world. The less you know, the worse the thing will work out."

"That's a long-winded way to say that only experts should be making things," snapped the woman, and Nepomuk couldn't help but agree.

But how could you enforce this when even a child was able to build a gigantic amusement park in a matter of heart beats?

"We need a mayor and a police force, and a city planner to structure this chaos, otherwise people could come to harm or die out there," continued the woman.

"I don't think they could die, again, but otherwise I agree that some order would be good," said Nepomuk.

As they were arguing, they didn't notice how the light that had previously streamed in without interruption seemed to diminish.

"What is going on out there?" asked Enya. She peeked through the blinds again and saw a massive shadow covering the market.

The group of elderly and Enya pushed outside to find several houses growing like beansprouts around the amusement park. Before they could exchange a single word, a magnified voice echoed across the city, for the town had grown even larger.

"Everyone, listen up. All this unconsidered creation must stop. We have all died and we all deserve a peaceful afterlife."

Nepomuk had heard this voice before.

"Who are you?" shouted someone.

"My name is Knight Lukas, and I'm afraid I started all of this. Mea culpa."

A stage with a sound system and lightshow rose behind the market stalls until it was about three metres above the ground and everyone on the banks could see the speaker.

"I understand that it is very exciting and tempting to make everything you want, but look around you. Is this really how you want to spend eternity? In a pile of junk?"

There was a murmur of agreement.

"What do you propose?" someone else shouted.

The crowd surged towards the stage and people who still dared to continue their conversation were quickly shushed.

"There you go, finally someone who is taking matters seriously," whispered the argumentative old woman.

"We need order, we need a vision for this place, we need a strong leader, and I am willing to sacrifice myself to take on the doubtlessly gruelling task of sorting things out."

The crowd gave some reserved applause and cheers here and there, though some people were positively enthusiastic. The old woman swung her fist in the air and jeered as if she were at a massive save-the-world demonstration.

"No, not him," whispered Enya, her cheeks glowing. "He's a rapist with neither morals nor kindness."

"What do you know," sneered the old woman. "You don't look old enough to have suffered even a day in your life."

"Enya is correct; he's not the right person to hold any power," said Nepomuk. "At least the people should have choice."

Knight Lukas strutted around the edge of the stage, shooting cannons with bloodcurdling bangs in all directions. Thousands upon thousands of banknotes came down over the masses.

After initial screaming and ducking from the loud noise, people started to scramble to fill their pockets with the paper money.

Without really knowing what he was doing, Nepomuk imagined a tower akin to a raised hide for hunters, which immediately rose from the ground and lifted him into the air.

"People of the afterlife!" shouted Nepomuk, but no one heard him.

Someone tapped him on the leg, and he saw Enya halfway up the tower passing him a megaphone.

"People of the afterlife!" he shouted again and this time, he had their attention. "Don't let yourself be fooled by shallow words and offerings that mean nothing here. You don't need money because you don't need anything."

"Maybe we don't need things, but we want them!" came a shout from somewhere.

Nepomuk felt dizzy. He had never done anything like this in his life. Enya nodded encouragingly from below.

"Then there shouldn't be anyone to stop you from acquiring them. It just needs to happen in an ordered way."

"That's what he said!"

"And he is correct, he is just not the right person to enforce and oversee any of it," said Nepomuk.

"But you are?" retorted Knight Lukas from across the sea of heads.

"Maybe not, but I led a life of decency and compassion. I died from cancer surrounded by my family."

"So did I," snivelled the old man from the bottom of Nepomuk's stand, and quiet empathy came from the largely elderly crowd.

"Maybe you'd care to tell us how you died, Mister Lukas?" shouted Nepomuk. He knew this was a low blow but might be effective.

"I died of grief and self-loathing over what my life had become," came the self-deprecating answer, and the people loved it.

Why could bad guys never unmask themselves? Nepomuk swayed between exposing this criminal and fighting a fair argument.

"Then what do you propose doing if you become leader of this settlement?" asked Nepomuk instead and apologized quietly to Enya who looked up at him accusingly.

"I will make sure that everyone has their own space to create whatever they want. We will have streets that are clean, shops that offer only the highest-quality merchandise, we will create jobs for everyone, and community spaces for parents and children."

The crowd murmured in surprise and Nepomuk knew why: who wanted a job in Paradise? He'd also advertised to the wrong cohort; most of the crowd were elderly. But Knight Lukas didn't seem to see his mistake. And then he made the ultimate fallacy of alienating even the smallest minority of the crowd: the young children.

"We will remove the junk from our town, remove unsafe buildings, remove eyesores that spoil the view, and we'll start with this hazardous amusement park."

"No!" came the response from hundreds or even thousands of children.

Nepomuk took his chance. "We cannot and should not stifle anyone's creativity. If we want this place, this town, this city to be a paradise for everyone, we need structures that allow everyone to thrive, from the children to the ancient." Nepomuk felt his blood rushing in his ears mixed with the sound of thousands of feet stomping and hands clapping in agreement.

"You are too old to lead this town," came a feeble attempt from Knight Lukas to diminish his approval.

"I have never felt better! You forget something: age doesn't mean anything here; it is what's in your heart that counts. You have told lies upon lies, covered up what you did during your lifetime, manipulated others in your lust for power, and all your actions have only cemented your self-indulgence. Whose mansion is that on the hill? Who would be the only one profiting from the view that you consider spoiled by a child's dream? You are not and never were a knight in shining armour."

The crowd was now positively on Nepomuk's side, but Knight Lukas had not surrendered yet. As if to prove

Nepomuk wrong, he stepped to the edge of his stage, gleaming in knight's armour.

"Well then, if it is the spectacle of dreams that will swing the vote here, I challenge you to a duel to the death."

What was wrong with this guy? Did he think he was Julius Ceasar? That he could rule with bread and circuses?

"And seeing that you are already dead, old man, you will be banned from this city upon your loss."

At least he had finally grasped what afterlife meant. However, the threat of being banned sunk deep into Nepomuk's heart. If he had to leave, he would be moving further and further away from finding Blanka again. He didn't know what was waiting out there and where his path would lead him. People left in all directions. Here he at least knew that she must arrive on the shoreline.

"I am not a violent man," began Nepomuk, his mind racing, "and I do not think that the spectacle of a man-on-man fight is the right way to settle this matter."

"Coward!" shouted several people.

"Oh, come on. You don't really want to go down the route of democratic elections? That would take ages to organize! A quick and dirty duel would solve things immediately, and we could all get on with our lives, deaths, afterlives, whatever," proposed Knight Lukas.

"You could nominate someone to fight on your behalf," suggested someone.

"Sure, I'm happy with that," sneered Knight Lukas, who had manifested a shiny broadsword.

This was ridiculous. Nepomuk didn't want to fight and certainly not in something that seemed to have become a medieval jousting competition. At what point would they stop? They couldn't kill each other.

"And who is to declare the winner?" asked Nepomuk.

"We fight until one of us gives up. How about *chicken* as a safe word," suggested Knight Lukas. He broke into a clanging chicken dance that garnered him several laughs.

Nepomuk had hoped to be able to install a jury, but the crowd seemed to favour the more spectacular version.

"And what weapons are allowed?"

"Anything you want; anything you can imagine."

Knight Lucas held his sword with both hands near his crotch and made it grow in size until he had to lean back to hold its weight.

"Any rules?"

"None."

Nepomuk had thought so and the cheers from the crowd told him that this was what had to happen. Talk about peer pressure. Nepomuk would never have dreamt, alive or dead, that he would have to engage in a sword fight at seventy-seven years of age to please a mob of geriatric zombies, for lack of a better word, and stop them from falling prey to an amoral banker.

He had one last option, though, as he definitely did not feel up to any sort of fighting. "Can I have a volunteer to fight on my behalf?"

A silence fell over the throng; everyone was listening for a voice to speak up. After all, most of this congregation of by-gones was not much younger than Nepomuk.

"I'll do it!" sounded a small voice from the midst of the crowd.

Chapter 9

THE CROWD PARTED TO let the volunteer through to Nepomuk's hide.

"Danilo!" gasped Nepomuk when he finally made out the six-year-old who was approaching his hide with steps that would have been earth-shaking if he had been a grown man but appeared merely as prolonged taps with his bare feet.

"Where are your shoes?" whispered Nepomuk when the boy had climbed to his height.

"What?" Danilo looked down at his feet. "Oh, I took them off to climb up the slide better."

"I can't let you do this."

"Why not?"

"Because you are just a child."

"So? You are a granddad?"

"Yes, but he is a strong man in freaking armour." Nepomuk gestured at Knight Lukas, who was leaning amused on the hilt of his sword watching the unlikely pair argue.

"So what? I made this!" Danilo pointed at the amusement park. "He made that." And then at the marble mansion that seemed dwarfed and boring in comparison.

He had a point. If this place let you create anything, then the person with the larger imagination had a huge advantage, and Nepomuk would have bet his last pair of underpants on a child rather than an unsuccessful businessman.

"Alright," he finally said. "But there is no shame in losing. We'll find another way to get rid of him if we need to."

"I'm not gonna lose," said Danilo with a cheerful smile.

"All I'm saying is, it is alright. And remember, the safe word is *chicken*."

"But I'm not gonna lose. I'm gonna win."

"Alright. I have accepted the generous offer by Danilo to fight on my behalf," shouted Nepomuk through the megaphone.

"Are you serious, old man? You're sending a child into battle?" came back the knight's response.

"You're gonna be toast!" shouted Danilo and the crowd broke out in laughter on hearing his tiny voice.

"We have discussed his proposition and he has made a very good argument that he will be able to beat you fair and square," said Nepomuk.

"Your choice, but I just want to remind everyone here, he is the one who sent the boy to his doom. I wash my hands of anything that might happen."

"Stop talking, you stinky tuna box!" shouted Danilo and this time grabbed the megaphone so that everyone could hear him.

Soon after, a large circle had been cleared and people imagined high stands where formerly crumbling abandoned market stalls had been.

"Are you sure about this?" asked Nepomuk as they stood in the shade beneath the stands behind a great wooden door that led into the arena. Knight Lukas didn't have to tell him that it was immoral to send a child into battle, and Nepomuk felt bitter remorse at this arrangement.

"Yes, I will protect you and Enya because you are my friends," replied Danilo and his brave innocence punched Nepomuk right in the stomach.

"I can't let you do that," said Nepomuk and closed the boy in a hug. "I will fight myself."

At that point the gate opened, and like a worm, Danilo wriggled out of Nepomuk's arms and sped into the arena where he was greeted with thunderous applause.

"Danilo, come back here!" called Nepomuk after the boy.

By the time he reached the gate, it was already closing. Nepomuk caught a last glimpse of Danilo, who waved at him happily whilst a larger-than-life knight entered the arena behind him.

"What have I done?" Nepomuk asked Enya and both hastened up the stairs to see what was happening.

"You can't catch me," Nepomuk heard Danilo's jolly voice from the depths of the arena as he pushed his way to the front.

The crowd cheered and laughed as Danilo ran circles around Knight Lukas, who was very slow to turn in his heavy armour. The hollering rose when Danilo's feet stopped touching the ground and he flew at dazzling speed around the knight, who swung his sword at him furiously.

The boy was almost too fast for his own good when he finished an entire circle around his contender only to stop abruptly in front of the blade that had been aimed at him a round earlier. Danilo shot straight up into the air and somersaulted over the head of the knight to twist his helmet back to front as revenge.

Finally, Knight Lukas accepted that he hadn't chosen the most useful form of armour and began throwing his helmet, chest and arm pieces to the side while Danilo sat down cross-legged to give his opponent time to prepare himself again.

This time, Knight Lucas forwent all protective gear and simply pulled out a Walter PPK as he marched towards Danilo in a black tuxedo. As soon as the boy got up, Knight Lukas fired his entire magazine at him, and if this had been the world of the living, Danilo would have been peppered with bullets. But this was the afterlife and Danilo understood better than most the infinite rules and possibilities of the place. In slow motion, he bent, twisted and landed back again on the floor, cinematically avoiding even being scratched by a single shot.

As soon as Danilo landed, his outfit changed into that of a cowboy. He even managed to display some of the features of John Wayne before he drew his revolver and shot a single bullet at his enemy's head.

Knight Lukas stopped stunned as a suction cup arrow stuck to his forehead and a little red flag with a chicken on it unravelled over his nose. Danilo broke out into raucous laughter joined by the thousands of spectators.

Enraged by the humiliation, Knight Lukas threw his weapon into the sand and began heaving heavily. His tuxedo ripped at the seams and the buttons on his white shirt popped off one by one to reveal an outrageously muscular upper body, but he somehow forgot to adapt his legs, so he looked like a bodybuilder who had never heard of leg day.

Danilo looked impressed and accepted the challenge on the spot. He grew instantly to a height of five metres, allowing him to look over even the highest ranks of the arena. His jawline became more prominent, his hair was gelled back again, and he wore a golden spandex suit with a cape. Again, he looked like a mutated cross between himself and all the superheroes he admired mixed with a good dash of Mexican wrestler.

Knight Lukas stopped in his tracks and looked at this superhuman child who laughed down at him with his two milk teeth missing at the front.

"Are you ready to fly?" thundered Danilo's childish voice over the plain. And then he picked up Knight Lukas, who flapped his arms around frantically.

"Say chicken," Danilo said as he swung the businessman around a couple of times only to release him at the highest point and fling him far into the distance.

The crowd went wild. Nepomuk and Enya rushed to embrace Danilo, who had transformed back into his little self.

"You were absolutely brilliant," gushed Enya.

"I know," grinned Danilo.

"What now?" asked Enya.

"Now comes an even harder task," said Nepomuk and raised his megaphone again. "People of the afterlife. I think it is abundantly clear that Danilo has won."

Nepomuk held Danilo's right hand and raised it, to the cheers of the deceased.

"As much as we all enjoyed this spectacle, this fight was supposed to find a leader to make this place safer and more enjoyable for everyone. It should be somewhere for all to come together and be led by the community rather than by a single person. If you are interested in being a creative member and overseeing some of the tasks ahead, please come to the bakery at the centre of the shore.

"For now, in case you haven't noticed it yet, this place is ruled only by your imagination. You are the creators of the world around you. However, here are some observations I have made. Your creations are only as good as the knowledge that you acquired during your lifetime. If you want quality, you will still need to find a master. Creations that are not used or abandoned will quickly fall into disrepair and eventually crumble back into the dust they were made from. Nonetheless, be mindful of others if you create something. I suggest that larger items should only be made several hundreds of metres away from the last building; houses and shops need to follow a plan and shouldn't be built too close to the shoreline to allow the new arrivals space to disembark. I suggest that no settlements should be closer to the river than the current boundary formed by the bakery, café and saloon. Lastly, time is unpredictable. There is neither night nor day, and neither will you feel tired, thirsty or hungry, but you can still indulge in these activities. As you will all have noticed, your memories are crystal clear, and I suggest that you take some time to reminisce about your life."

Nepomuk wasn't sure whether anybody would follow his words, but he felt that he had done his duty. He hoped that his appeal regarding riparian developments fell on fertile soil, as this meant that Blanka would see their bakery when she arrived. He also hoped that instead of mindlessly creating things, the dearly departed calmed down in their zeal for mundane possessions, making this place a more relaxed and peaceful dwelling.

Voices broke out from the ranks shouting questions.

"If you'd like to help organize this place and have suggestions regarding its development, please see me at the bakery," shouted Nepomuk, but he already had the feeling that things would get difficult, judging by the aggression in the tone of the questioners.

Nepomuk, Enya and Danilo cleaved a way through the crowd that was closing in on them. Danilo collected teddy bears and love hearts from all sides and seemed to mature under the admiration.

By the time they arrived at the bakery, Danilo had grown into the man he would have become had he not fallen down that well and hit his head. Still, he didn't look quite right, just like his superhero creations.

"Hey, do you wanna hear a joke?" asked Danilo as he turned around to the fans who followed them all the way.

Several women swooned and batted their eyes at him, and Nepomuk admitted than Danilo had grown into a rather handsome young man. But still, something was off.

"What do you get if you cross a potato with a superhero? Spuderman."

Danilo broke out into a rather unmanly cackle and Nepomuk suddenly knew what was off. The boy had created himself after the man that he thought he could have become, but without the actual life experience, he was still just a little boy in a grown man's body.

"Come on," said Nepomuk and placed a hand on Danilo's shoulder. "You should save some of your jokes for later."

"But I know hundreds of them," assured Danilo. "What do you call a chicken crossed with a cow?"

"I don't know," answered Nepomuk, and thought that he should probably feel tired right now.

"A roast beef," laughed Danilo as he was gently pushed inside.

"What?"

"A roast beef."

"Do you mean a roost beef?" asked Enya helpful.

"Yes, that's what I said."

For the rest of what felt like the evening to a very long day, people of all ages went in and out of the little bakery, not to buy bread, but to provide their five cents on how this place should look and what should be allowed and what not. The suggestions, or often outright demands, included one for good free coffee, with the emphasis on 'good'. It came from someone who constantly referred to Nepomuk as 'mate'. Another popular one was no children's noise between six and eight in the morning, two hours around lunch time, and in the evening from five o'clock until six the next morning. Nepomuk pointed out, again, that there was no day or night, and everybody would be living according to their own times. This yielded him a severe berating, one that included a cane stick with a knife hidden in the handle. Luckily, Danilo was still in his saviour mode and ushered the old lady outside, telling another joke on the way.

Despite these rather impolite encounters, Nepomuk's first order was to build a belltower with a large clock to synchronize everyone's activities and allow for more precise meetings. He did not, however, stipulate that children should be quiet at specific times and hoped that everyone, young and old, would just find some grace and charity.

With a rather small group of people who actually volunteered to help, he agreed on distances between buildings that also allowed for streets and alleys in between. The troupe then went out to mark the streets with ropes, so that new structures could be created on either side. He still made sure that no new buildings would be erected between his bakery and the river.

Nepomuk felt that they had made good progress and that solid foundations had been laid for the settlement to flourish without much further intervention, but the people of the afterlife felt differently. The doorbell would not stop ringing, and the tone of conversations got more and more impolite the more outrageous the demands were. If Nepomuk pointed out that volunteering would be very much appreciated, the responses turned outright rude.

"I did not work my entire life just to continue even after my death!"

"I demand a chef, a maid, a gardener who can also clean my pool, and a chauffeur, but I can do without the maid and the gardener until tomorrow."

Whilst Nepomuk couldn't provide these people with their demands, which garnered him the threat of a lawyer, he did arrange for noticeboards on every corner where people could advertise their services, if they wished to do so.

Eventually, Enya disabled the doorbell and turned the sign to 'closed', which lessened the influx of concerned citizens, but it was only when they moved into the bakehouse, where they couldn't be seen from the shop window, that people stopped coming in.

"I don't think I'm made out for this," confessed Nepomuk.

"I never thought politics was so difficult," said Enya.

"I think it's just boring," said Danilo, who looked again like a six-year-old as he popped Herman's bubbles with a wooden spatula.

"Maybe now that we have a structure, we can have some form of election," suggested Nepomuk.

"Boring," whinged Danilo.

"Or maybe some committees that deal with things," said Enya.

Danilo sighed.

"That's a good idea. Let's make a list," said Nepomuk. "The quicker I have them off my back the better."

He created pen and paper, but before he could put the first name down, Danilo interrupted.

"I wanna go home," said the boy quietly. "I miss my mama and papa."

Chapter 10

NEPOMUK AND ENYA LOOKED at Danilo, who was listlessly stirring Herman. He had always looked so energetic, with not a care in the world, but the truth was that Danilo was a little boy who had lost his parents, and his parents had lost him, way too early.

They sat down with him, and Enya poured some flour and sugar into the jar to feed Herman.

"I'm sure your parents miss you very much," said Nepomuk.

"I wanna go home," said Danilo and he started to cry helplessly.

"Come here," said Nepomuk and opened his arms. The child accepted and crawled into his embrace.

Nepomuk rocked Danilo until the wailing stopped.

"Do you want to tell me about your parents?" asked Nepomuk.

The boy shook his head, buried in Nepomuk's chest. "I love them so much," said Danilo, nonetheless. "My mama had made pancakes for our picnic, and I didn't get any. Pancakes are my favourite."

"I like pancakes too," said Nepomuk.

"My mama always made them with blueberries and sugar."

"That's a good combination."

"She also made good bread, much better than yours."

"I'm sure we'd have been friends," smiled Nepomuk.

"I don't know what to do now."

"Well, what would you like to do?"

"Nothing."

"Would you like to go on your loop-de-loop?"

"No."

"Would you like to go to the cinema?"

"Too loud."

"How about a swimming pool."

"I said I don't know what I wanna do." Danilo pushed away from Nepomuk. "Why can't I just go home?"

"I'm afraid even when you are dead, you can only move in one direction."

"That's not true; I can move wherever I want."

"What I mean is you cannot go back to being alive once you have died."

"Why not?"

"That's just how it is. Just like you cannot become younger again when you are old."

"That is so unfair."

"I know."

"What did people do before this place?" asked Enya suddenly. "I mean, when I arrived here, there was nothing and you made something out of nothing; you started it. But where did people go before that?"

Nepomuk felt their eyes on him.

"I don't know. People just kept on walking in all directions."

"But where did they go?"

"I don't know. No-one ever came back to tell me, and I never left these shores."

"So maybe there is a way back if you only move forward," suggested Enya.

"Maybe." Nepomuk had never thought about that.

"Why are you still here?" asked Danilo.

"Because I am hoping to find my wife."

"Is she alive or dead?"

"I hope she is still alive."

"Why? Don't you want her to come and get you?"

"I do, with all my heart. That's why I'm still here – so she can find me. But if she's dead already that means I have missed her."

Nepomuk's heart sank. There was a real possibility that Blanka had already passed by and with all the kerfuffle going on today (or had it already been a year?), there was no guarantee that he had not missed her.

"Maybe we can go together?" suggested Danilo hopeful.

Nepomuk smiled wistfully. As much as he feared that Blanka had moved on without him, he was sure in his heart that she was still alive and well.

"I wish I could come with you, but I can't – at least not yet," admitted Nepomuk.

"That's okay. I mean, your wife must be old already, so I'm sure she won't be long. But I don't think my parents will come soon, so I must go to them."

"But where will you go?" said Enya, almost fearful.

"Just that way," said Danilo and pointed in a random direction.

"Let me pack you some bread," said Nepomuk and got back up.

He went into the store, but came back empty-handed. They were still out of everything and hadn't had time to make more yet. But there was one loaf left.

"Here," he said and handed Danilo the fruit loaf that he had retained for Blanka.

Enya looked at him with big eyes.

"I'll make another one," he reassured her.

"This smells good, almost as good as my mother's," said Danilo, and Nepomuk and Enya laughed at the insulting innocence of the child.

"And when you run out you can make yourself some new bread," said Enya and got busy creating another jar, which she filled with a quarter of Herman. "Don't forget to feed him, then when you are hungry you can either make bread with some more flour or maybe some pancakes."

"Pancakes. Thank you," said Danilo beaming.

They walked the boy outside and were pleasantly surprised that their area had somewhat quietened down. The market stalls had well and truly crumbled back to dust so that they could see the river again.

The edge of the settlement was not far, but had grown in other places, mainly upwards, as the street markings that Nepomuk's city-planning squad had outlined were obeyed.

Danilo had imagined himself the outfit of a cowboy again, complete with spurs and a holster. Then he swung a long stick over his shoulder onto which he had fastened a red checked cotton handkerchief that contained his provisions.

"Hey, what did the cowboy say at his second rodeo?" asked Danilo, grinning.

"Go on?"

"This ain't my first."

They all laughed, but Danilo laughed the loudest.

"I'm gonna miss you," said Enya, and kneeled to hug him.

"I'll miss you, too. Especially the young you, you know? The girl. She was great fun."

"Well, it's gonna be a whole lot less fun without you," said Enya earnestly, studying his face.

"I know. Try the bouncy castle when you miss me most."

"I will."

Danilo turned to the open plain and looked around.

"You should call this place La Plana."

Then, he licked his finger, held it into the windless air and began marching towards the horizon, his spurs softly jingling at every step.

"See you later alligator!" shouted Nepomuk.

"Don't forget your toilet paper!" shouted Danilo back at them.

The clock tower struck twelve for the first time when Nepomuk and Enya strolled back into town. Even though the streets followed an accurate checkerboard pattern, nothing was quite right, or at least nothing quite usual. The young barista who used to run the café next door to Nepomuk had opened a modern coffee joint that had large glass fronts. What was unusual about it was that it was raised a good metre above the ground and a mysterious fog made it appear as if it were floating. Nepomuk and Enya went inside to get themselves a coffee, which was the most exquisite that Nepomuk had ever tasted. Moreover, from the inside, the customers looked down on white clouds and the seats were soft white chairs that invited the customers to lounge and chat. The barista did not brew coffee or even serve anyone, but the customers simply came in and filled their cups from a counter akin to a bar where every tap held a different brew.

"This looks like heaven," said Nepomuk when the barista came over to greet them.

"That was the idea. Help yourself, everything is free. Pick a cup and when you are done, place it in the bins over there to be recycled."

"Is this fresh?" asked Nepomuk sceptically as the steaming brown gold filled his mug.

"As fresh as I can imagine it."

Enya added some coconut syrup and milk to her coffee, but Nepomuk enjoyed it black and felt his tastebuds pop and his spirits awaken as if twenty years had fallen from his shoulders.

"Another cup of this and I'll turn into a baby," joked Nepomuk. "This is what I was hoping this place could be. Everyone can do what they want without needing anything."

When they walked out onto the streets again, they saw that someone had built a spiral staircase onto the side of the café and opened a patisserie on top. It was built in the style of a romantic Tudor castle, complete with ivy foliage. Nepomuk wondered whether it was fake, as the ivy did not root into anything but just sprung directly from the wall.

As they were already there, they decided to try the place. Nepomuk found the most exquisite pastries and cakes that even he couldn't make better. Just as they never felt hungry, they also never felt full, and so they feasted on twelve different types of macarons, about half of which had flavours that Nepomuk had never tasted; a New York cheesecake that Enya found so good she 'wanted to have a bath in it'; small tarts that looked as though a carnival had exploded onto them; and finally a filled chocolate cake and an orange souffle that melted away in their mouths like candyfloss.

And off they walked again. The next block appeared to contain small shops that offered all sorts of handcrafted ornaments and toys, from glass-blown statues that defied gravity, to old-fashioned mechanicals that ticked and steamed, or even spat fire. Each shop was created in a different style and right next to each other, so you could see how much the owner understood about construction work. Nepomuk found a cuckoo clock like one his parents had possessed; however, the artist was not simply giving away his creations but offered them in exchange for a delivery of large-salted pretzels.

The first floors above the shops appeared mostly as private living quarters of the shopkeepers, though some had extended their apartments over other shops, which in turn had extended their living room to protrude out over the street. The further they walked into the heart of the city the more outrageous grew the solutions of people who hadn't found another space to create their shops or houses and didn't just want to live on the edge of town like a bourgeois suburb.

On one block there was an expertly constructed weatherboard house with a front garden on top of what looked like a Blockbuster video store, but what was more astounding was the perfectly balanced penthouse on top of its gable with a private glass elevator leading up on its side.

"I thought they went under years ago," pondered Enya, peering into the video rental store.

Nepomuk saw a group of people in their mid-twenties strolling through the aisles, wearing outdated eighties-style clothing mixed with the occasional comfortable item that they most likely acquired at a later age. They were probably all in their sixties or seventies when they died, but reminiscing about their favourite times in life, they looked youthful and glowing from excitement as they turned over VHS covers and read the descriptions.

The next blocks were even higher and looked like misshapen skyscrapers where each floor had a different builder.

Some blocks looked as if they leaned to one side only to be counterbalanced by a floor that protruded in the other direction.

There were cinemas and restaurants, bars and cafes, gyms and hairdressers; everything a modern city would offer and more.

Finally, they reached the heart of the city. Nepomuk was happy to see that the children of La Plana had kept Danilo's amusement park alive with the addition of a Ferris wheel, a haunted house, and hundreds of sweetshops that the children ran themselves. The sweets they sold were as outrageous as their fantasies could produce. There was candyfloss that made you exhale smoke when it melted, candied apples without the apple, hotdogs shaped to look like real dachshunds, and fizzy drinks that made you float into the air. Not that the children needed a drink for that after they had watched Danilo fight the knight. The children imagined themselves to have all sorts of superpowers; even a wizarding world could not have kept up with them.

However, they also came across abandoned shops and houses. Nepomuk wondered whether people had decided to start a new endeavour somewhere else in town or whether people were still deciding to leave for the unknown as Danilo had done. He was nonetheless pleased when he realized that Knight Lukas's marble mansion had been repurposed as the haunted house and that its derelict nature finally brought out its charm.

Nepomuk had seen enough for the day and wanted to go back to their bakery, but when he looked at Enya, she had turned back into a child and looked at the bouncy castle with yearning eyes.

"Go on," laughed Nepomuk. "A dignified farewell for our superhero."

Enya ran as undignified as only a child could run and disappeared with a loud roar into the squishy depths of the castle.

On his way back, Nepomuk found that something was still nagging him about the cityscape. It was only when he saw Enya's sunflowers that he realized what it was. There were no plants: there were no lawns or flowerbeds, and no trees along the streets. He had already realized that no one had created any pets and assumed that this special power of creating life was denied to the dead. But plants were living things and Enya had managed to create some. How had she done it?

The petals were still bright yellow and soft to the touch, but Nepomuk could already see the seeds forming on the disc floret. Still puzzled about Enya's creation, he went inside and was greeted by the comfortable and mundane silence of his empty shop. Deep in thought, he went to the back to make some more bread and rolls, considering trying out some more unusual flavours and combinations of flour and raising agents. But he felt dull and unimaginative after all the experiences in the city, and only stood there lost.

Then, his eye fell on the piece of paper that they had left behind to make a list of committees that would be useful to run the city.

He noted down a committee to oversee the creation and integrity of new and existing buildings as well as an administrative office where people should give notice if they abandoned a creation, especially when others were impacted by it, such as the floors above. Somehow, he couldn't come up with anything else. He felt uninspired and like a simpleton who only knew how to make bread and Sunday rolls.

The belltower droned twelve again and Nepomuk wondered whether it was broken or whether another twelve hours had already passed. Then he remembered the cuckoo clock he wanted to trade for pretzels and began to mix a yeast dough. While the dough was resting, he prepared the sodium carbonate lye to dip the pretzels in before baking, which gave them their typical brown colour and slightly soapy taste.

Chapter 11

NEPOMUK DIDN'T STOP AT making simple German pretzels with coarse salt sprinkled on top; he made variations using sesame seeds, twisted the dough, and added a filling of garlic butter or pizza sauce before forming the typical pretzel curl. Then, he moved on to elaborate braids, three-dimensional structures and finally made bite-size balls with mystery fillings.

He added hangings all around the walls of the bakery shop to display his work, yet he still didn't think his creations could keep up with any of the other shops in the city. He racked his brain to come up with new and wild recipes and made loaf after loaf and roll after roll until every basket, drawer, shelf, and cabinet was filled to the brim. Even the table, where Danilo had made the blueprint for his amusement park in gingerbread, was covered in baked goods.

Disheartened but needing space to keep going, he opened his shop for customers.

People started coming in as if he had turned on a giant magnet for the decease. At first, it was mainly individuals who had just arrived and who inquired more about where they were rather than wanting something to eat. Nepomuk patiently explained the rules of this side of the River Styx, pointing out that any new developments should follow the already existing grid of streets and that random creations should only take place outside of the city.

He had just packed the delivery for the cuckoo clock and started to wonder where the dearly departed were who had pestered him about rules and regulations when a familiar person entered. It was the old lady who had called for a mayor and police force, obnoxiously making suggestions and indirectly implying that someone else should carry them out immediately. To his surprise, the lady had actually come in to offer her services this time.

"I have founded the society for knitters and weavers, and we are providing guidance for and approval of quality wool products. I'm their president," she announced. "I think you could do with some help from someone with experience of running a community."

"That is very considerate," said Nepomuk as he served a customer. "I had some ideas in the same direction."

"Did you?"

"Yes. I was thinking that we needed committees to oversee the quality of products, especially buildings."

"My word, there are too many hazardous constructions out there, especially that rollercoaster. And did you know those little brats are now illegally occupying Mr Knight's mansion?"

"Mr Lukas, you mean."

Nepomuk actually thought the rollercoaster was one of the safest constructions in town as it was upheld by hundreds of children's minds.

"I mean Mr Lukas Knight, your opponent for mayor."

"His name was Knight Lukas, and I'm not sure whether he wanted to be a mayor or a despot."

"Really? His parents named him Knight?"

Apparently, this point weighed heavier on her dislike scale than the fact that Knight Lukas had tried to make himself an absolute monarch.

"I suggest we invite masters of their trade to oversee their particular industries. In order to assure that these so-called masters are actually up to the task, we should have them demonstrate their skills," she suggested.

"Sounds like a plan."

"Excellent. I've got my ladies waiting outside to start the recruitment process. We just wanted to have everything in order; that's why we asked you. As the mayor, you are obviously the head of the selection committee."

"Right," said Nepomuk, slightly uneasily.

"Could I get a pretzel?" asked a boy who could barely look over the counter.

"Yes. Oh, could you take this basket to the curiosity shop two blocks down? They have a clock for me. If you bring it back, you'll get a cinnamon swirl as well."

"Okay," said the boy and disappeared with the basket.

"You let a boy run errands for you?" asked the lady, and Nepomuk wondered whether this fell under child labour.

"I bet he'll eat them himself or give them to his friends at their amusement park."

Apparently, child labour was none of her concern.

"You should be more trusting; it makes things a lot easier," said Nepomuk.

"Only if you like disappointment," she snapped. "Anyway, we have already placed advertisements around town. Someone had the good idea to put up community noticeboards."

"That was me."

"Oh. Well, we specified that we're open for demonstrations from eight o'clock. Since there is no ante or post meridian here, we specified the one in three hours. That reminds me: I propose to have the belltower ring as a twenty-four-hour clock."

"I'm not sure how people would take it if the bell rang twenty-four times to indicate midnight."

"I think the advantage of knowing exactly what time it is outweighs the little bit of nuisance that a bell would make once every hour."

Nepomuk started losing his patience. "I shall see you in three hours then. I need to attend to my customers now."

"Good. And if you could clean up and make some space before then, that would be splendid. Oh, could I have one of these for the way?" she asked, pointing at some eclairs.

"Take them all. I'm sure your ladies outside would appreciate them."

"Really? How generous of you."

The lady finally bustled out of the bakery and Nepomuk took a deep breath.

Three hours later, he sat crammed in the middle of six more old ladies, four of whom were knitting things that looked like doilies or very elaborate wedding dresses for a frostbitten bride.

Even though he had cleaned up and made space as requested, the shop front was still rather limited, but no one seemed to notice.

"Righto, let's get started," said the lady, who seemed frighteningly in her element. "Marge, can you get the first one in?"

Marge, who sat nearest the window, put down a clipboard before guiding a man in who introduced himself as Matt White.

"Hello Matt, I'm Georgina, president of the knitters and weavers."

So that's her name, thought Nepomuk.

"This is our mayor." She graciously waved at Nepomuk, but her sparkle dimmed for a moment when she realized that she didn't know his name.

"Hello, I'm Nepomuk," he said. "Could we maybe not introduce me as the mayor? I know that's what you've been thinking I was, but really, I'm only a concerned citizen, just like you," Nepomuk whispered to Georgina, finally getting a huge weight off his chest.

"Well, if you are not the mayor, what are you doing here?"

"I'm a member of this committee to find suitable leaders for our industry trades."

"Well, no. You are only here because you are the mayor. Otherwise, I must ask you to leave. We don't want to open ourselves up to any charges of bribery or nepotism."

"There's no law court or police force that could enforce any punishment."

Matt White waited patiently as Nepomuk and Georgina argued in whispers.

"The court of public opinion is often more damaging than any jail sentence. But you are right; we should have police to protect us."

"From what?"

"Are you just here to argue?"

"No, I was here to see this gentlemen's skills because you invited me."

"But you are not a mayor." She looked around as if this were the first time she had seen the shop. "You are a baker, which is a trade that should be regulated. Have you proven to anyone that you are actually making genuine bread?"

"Are you kidding me? You were in here only three hours ago and saw me giving away my baked goods."

"You gave them away without any return service? That seems highly suspicious. Marge, note down that the new leader of the baker's guild needs to examine this shop."

"I'm a master baker. This bakery was the very first shop on this side of the shore."

"Do you have any proof of that?"

Just then the cuckoo in his new clock chimed two o'clock.

"Your clock is off," noted Georgina.

"There, I traded soft German pretzels today for this clock. You were here when I sent the boy out, who by the way did not eat them himself."

Georgina bristled dismissively. "Alright. I accept this as partial proof. Now, I suggest you get in line to demonstrate your skills or leave this committee meeting."

"This is my shop!"

"And I'm the president of the knitters and weavers."

"I'll leave," grumbled Nepomuk and squeezed out from between two knitters who by now had joined their projects so that Nepomuk had to dive underneath to get out.

As he went into his bakehouse, he heard Georgina ask Matt White sweetly to state his name, occupation, and what demonstration he intended to do.

"My name is Matt White," said Matt White. "I am, or rather *was*, from Tucson, Arizona, and I was a carpenter."

Nepomuk watched through the open door out of sight of any of the knitters and weavers.

"And what will you show us today?" asked Georgina as if she were talking to a child.

Matt White might have looked like a middle-aged man right now, but Nepomuk spotted the tell-tale signs of comfortable black leather shoes and the outline of suspenders under his thin jumper and guessed that Mr White was probably the same age as Georgina when he died.

"I like a challenge, so I would like to ask you ladies to request anything of me," smiled Matt White gingerly.

"Uh, you should be careful with such offerings," teased Georgina and Nepomuk cringed back into his bakery. "Well, for now, how about a Queen Anne coffee table?"

Matt White started to mime carving the bent legs, cutting an oval tabletop, and finally putting everything together. As he polished, the exquisite walnut table appeared and garnered approving whispers from the ladies.

"Very well done," praised Georgina. "We'll let you know as soon as we have seen all aspirants. How may we reach you?"

"I have a small shop three blocks down and one to the left from here, and a flat on the fifth and a half floor."

"Marge, write that down. Also make a note that we need street names and house numbers."

Nepomuk smiled quietly. At least these were not his problems anymore.

"Shall I take the table?" asked Matt White.

"No, leave it. We might need it to compare pieces later."

Nepomuk wondered whether Georgina was just trying to nab some nice furniture, as there was surely not enough space in his shop to keep every item that was about to come into existence.

The next person made a children's toy, but Georgina faulted it because it had too many removable parts that were a choking hazard for infants.

Nepomuk decided that he would start another batch of fruit loaves and replace the one he had held back for Blanka, so she would get a fresh one when she arrived.

Then, he wrapped his mind again around new creations and made a salty dough that he would fill with sweet jam and cover in chocolate.

When he peered out to the front again, he saw a beautiful glass vase in the shape of a swan, a wooden jewellery box (Matt White clearly had some competition in town), a set of Chinese teacups, one of which was filled with chocolate pralines, and finally a man who was building a brick wall right in the middle of his bakery shop. He only hoped they would make him take that wall apart again once he was done. Georgina could obviously not take that one home with her.

Disappointed, Nepomuk found that his latest creation turned out to be chocolate-glazed doughnuts, although the saltiness of the dough gave it a little twist. At least his fruit loaves were masterpieces; simple but perfect. He fed Herman before embarking on the creation of Sunday rolls that included all the seeds known to mankind. They turned out to be so dense and heavy that he had to soak them in milk before he could chew them. Despite all, they made an interesting base for the weird New York carrot cheesecake that he attempted next.

The bakehouse filled up quickly. Eventually, Nepomuk could do nothing more than sit on a small stool in front of the oven door, which was the only space left for him. With nothing else to do, he wished he had a book. Maybe one of the ladies had a spare pair of knitting needles and he could pick up a new hobby, but they were still busy out there.

Then he had an idea. He could make himself a book, but when he had drawn a square on the floor and imagined a pirate adventure book, he quickly found that the story was pieced together from all the books he remembered from his lifetime, which made for a partially interesting read but mostly didn't make any sense at all.

He didn't dare go outside for fear of attracting Georgina's wrath, even though he knew that was ridiculous as this was still his shop. How long could this go on for? Surely, the front was just as full as the back by now. Just then he heard glass shattering and jumped up to see what had happened.

The ladies all stood behind the counter as a man broke down his shop window with a sledgehammer.

"No!" Nepomuk screamed but was held off by Georgina's stern call to stand back.

"What is he doing?" he shouted agitatedly.

"He's making a greenhouse," explained Georgina matter-of-factly.

"But I don't want a greenhouse attached to my shop!"

"It's not about you, but if you ask me, this will give your shop a much greater appeal."

The man was now sweeping up the shards. He had swivelled the chairs around on which the committee had sat and placed them in pairs in his extension, a steel construction out of keeping with the shop.

"What have you done?" Nepomuk asked the builder once he was finished, and it was safe to step forward. He almost fell over the brick wall that was still standing rather solidly in the middle of the shop.

"I'm applying for the role of guild master for greenhouses, and this is the closest I could come up with given the limited space. The angles of the windows allow for optimal sun exposure. If it gets too hot, you can open these shutters and let down these blinds. You can probably get someone to make you higher-quality blinds, but that's not really my area of expertise."

"But ..." Nepomuk was lost for words. "Are there even people ... can you even make plants? And what about the sun? There is no sun!"

"Now, now. I can see that you are quite upset, but these are secondary questions," interrupted Georgina and moved with her ladies to inspect the greenhouse extension.

"It looks very well made; however, the demolition of the original shop window could have been done with a few more safety precautions."

Nepomuk followed them into the glass box, still in disbelief. He felt like a cupcake on display. The only thing missing was a rotating floor so that consumers could see him from all sides.

"Thank you very much for your time. We will get back to you with our decision as soon as possible," said Georgina. Marge noted down the man's contact details. He lived in a subterranean cave dug into the hill of the marble mansion ghost house, rather a stark contrast for a greenhouse builder.

"Here, I recommend this builder should you make the unfortunate decision to return to your original and outdated shop design."

Georgina handed Nepomuk a business card written in Marge's handwriting.

Just as he looked up from Mister Rudransh Kumar's name, he saw Enya stumbling towards the shop through his recently acquired jutting window front.

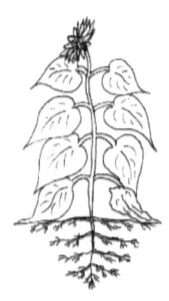

Chapter 12

ENYA WAS NO LONGER the little girl whom Nepomuk had left but, to his worry, she looked just like she did on the day they had met. She stumbled and hit her knee hard on the ground. Nepomuk hurried out of his shop, shouting back to the knitters and weavers that he'd be closing now.

Tears ran from Enya's eyes and left lines in her dusty face.

"What happened?" asked Nepomuk as he guided her back inside.

Enya was about to answer when she blinked away more tears and looked at the women in the shop who were folding a giant knitted sunshade.

"Thank you for hosting us tonight. We'll probably have a second round of guild selection soon to fill the positions of master baker, master conductor, master of ceremony, and high priest. Considering that you are not, and never were, the mayor, we'll probably look for a different place," said Georgina. "Oh, and I'll be sending someone to pick up all of these exhibits."

Nepomuk and Enya waited in silence until the last lady had packed up her knitting needles and left. Before the next person could enter, Nepomuk turned the sign to 'closed'.

"What happened?" asked Nepomuk again, but whilst Enya had been ready to blurt out her answer before, she had now composed herself enough to mull over what she wanted to share.

He knew that pause and the downward look before giving an answer. It usually meant that words were carefully weight to shroud the maybe ugly truth.

"What happened here?" she asked instead.

Ah, the attempt to sidestep one topic by opening another.

"We got an extension to our shop and the knitters and weavers held job interviews for guild leaders," Nepomuk replied.

"Is this still a bakery or an antiques shop?" She picked up a Chinese teacup and placed it carefully back on its saucer.

Nepomuk pulled a wrought-iron table and two chairs from the pile of demonstration pieces. One chair was exquisitely carved with ivy twines around its legs and a little mouse hiding between the leaves; the other poured from liquid red plastic directly into a seat-shaped sculpture.

He sat down on the plastic chair and was surprised by how comfortable it was.

"Have a seat," he suggested.

Enya perched down on the brick wall.

"Now, what happened to make you cry?" asked Nepomuk for the third time, and Enya began crying again.

"I guess you could say that my memories caught up with me," she finally sobbed.

Nepomuk waited patiently.

"There are not just good people here, you know; bad people die too, and they come to the same place," she explained.

Nepomuk had wondered about that, though he wouldn't have classed Georgina as a bad person. Maybe Knight Lukas. No, *definitely* Knight Lukas after what he had done to Enya.

He felt how his throat closed realizing what kind of bad people Enya might be referring to.

"Did someone hurt you?" he asked, with rising blood pressure.

Enya nodded silently.

"Who was it?"

He didn't know how to approach the potentially horrific topic. Should he just call it by its name or wait until she confirmed what had happened? And then what? There were no police they could go to, nor were there any effective punishments that could be laid out. Maybe he could challenge the perpetrator to a duel. He had read Superman comics as a child; he should be able to muster enough imagination to defeat even the strongest opponent. But then, so far, his imagination had only been sufficient to make chocolate-glazed doughnuts and a slightly altered version of a cheesecake.

"How about you start from when I left?" suggested Nepomuk and felt guilty for having left her alone in the first place.

"Okay. I first went on the bouncy castle, just like Danilo suggested. It was great. There is an inflatable dragon in the dungeon that alternately spits foam and water. The kids love it, and they get clean. I bet it was an adult who came up with it. Then I went on the rollercoaster, which was a perfect way to get dry again. I even went into Knight Lukas's mansion. His bedroom was left unchanged, and I think it was the most frightening room in the house.

"I had something to eat and then I decided to sleep for a bit and dream about my early childhood. I didn't know I used to be so happy. When I woke up, someone had built a swing carousel but with spaceships instead of chairs and they turned in all directions, literally. And then someone put bumper cars on the paths to get around."

Nepomuk wondered how much time had passed. To him, it felt like day, but by the sounds of it a week seemed more like it.

"And then I had a little accident with my bumper car. Nothing bad; I just crashed through a wall of hay balls. A man pulled me out and asked me where to get the best sweets. I showed him and as a thank you, he offered me one of his sweets. It was a little white pill with a smiley on it. And then he told me he knew other places to have fun."

"You were a child," puffed Nepomuk.

"I guess I must have looked fourteen. That was when I drove my first real car. Coincidentally, I also landed in a ditch that time."

"Still a child!"

Enya looked at him with a mixture of amusement at his indignation and sadness because he was right.

"Anyway," she continued quietly. "I went with him. At first it was fun. Great fun. There are dozens of underground clubs that are all connected through tunnels, so you wouldn't know about them. Almost like a village. I don't know; I must have been in there for a week or so. You can really get lost. Every club has its own theme and music, and there are bars with drinks I have never heard of. But one thing was exactly the same and that's drug dealers. I couldn't resist," she croaked.

Nepomuk took her into his arm, and she cried like the day they met.

"It all came back again. I knew what I was doing, but I couldn't stop myself."

"You did the right thing and walked away. Do you remember who hurt you?"

"Yes and no. One club looked like hell, and I mean like the hot, fire and flames thing. There were demons, or people who looked like demons, I don't know. They branded people with their logo. Someone held me down."

"Can I see? We can use it to identify them," said Nepomuk eagerly.

"It was on my bottom."

"Oh."

"And it's already healed again. That's the good thing, or bad. Nothing you do stays for long, at least not physically. Even the drugs wore off extremely quickly. But there are an awful lot of spiked drugs and very bad trips, and people who take advantage of you when you are most vulnerable."

"These clubs or dungeons or whatever they are should be outlawed. Let's go and find the knitters and weavers."

"The knitters and weavers? Do you really think a group of grannies are the right people for this?"

"Don't be pejorative."

"Sorry. But what are they gonna do? Poke them with their knitting needles? I don't think they can do anything."

"I think there are probably very few people here who want to cross Georgina. She appears to be very resistant to the temptation of drugs and has kind of a secret touch when it comes to unruly people."

He searched his pockets and the counter for an address for the knitters' club house, but all he found was Rudransh Kumar's business card.

"If only I knew how to find them," he muttered. "Let's look at the noticeboard on the corner. I'm sure they—"

"No."

"But this needs to be stopped. People are getting hurt."

"Yes, but maybe they like it."

"Did you like it?"

"At first."

Nepomuk stared at her. Was she really letting other people go through her experiences without caring for any of them?

"I don't think there is anything you can do. These people will just move on to somewhere else and how would you even stop anyone from just making their own drugs? I mean, isn't this what this place is about? Total freedom?"

"But only as long as that freedom doesn't infringe upon anyone else's freedom."

"Look, I'll go with you and even try to show you how to get to the clubs, but not right now."

"But people are getting hurt!"

"Some people like that."

"Children could be lured into this morass."

"It's not like they can die here."

"No, but even if your physical harm heals pretty quickly, you can still sustain wounds to your soul. You said it yourself."

"Who are you? The upholder of moral standards?" shouted Enya and Nepomuk saw himself confronted with a rowdy teenager.

"No, all I'm upholding is simple decency!" he shouted back.

"Not everyone needs saving!"

"Maybe not, but some people, like yourself, sometimes don't know what is good for them."

"You know, you are not my dad!" She stormed out of the shop.

How did this conversation turn so quickly?

He saw her through his display window marching straight to the river and slumping down at its shore. He somehow felt that he didn't want to be responsible for anyone here in the afterlife. Everyone had their chance to make their experiences in life, make mistakes and learn from them, and this place allowed everyone to remember exactly what these lessons were so they could move on and not make the same mistakes again. She was right: he was not her father, nor did he want to be.

He could see that she had obviously had a troubled and rather short life, and maybe she didn't have the time to learn from her mistakes. Maybe her only option was to repeat her mistakes and have a second chance to work it out without having to fear the worst consequences anymore. By the looks of it though, she didn't want to learn from her mistakes, and she didn't care about others falling into the same traps.

Nepomuk suddenly realized that maybe she just wanted as little responsibility for anyone else as he wanted. Sometimes, it was more than enough to look after oneself, and sometimes you didn't even manage that.

He started to feel sorry for her again and knew, as much as he wished it wasn't like that, he cared for her. Then he saw that Enya had waded into the river.

Nepomuk stormed out, fell, got up again and ran until the river covered his knees.

"Enya! Don't do it. I will help you; I am here, and we can get through this together."

She was still moving forward without even acknowledging that she had heard him, and then she dropped and disappeared.

Nepomuk took a deep breath and dived to where he had seen her last. He took several powerful strokes underwater in the direction of where he felt the river was flowing and found her foot. With his last strength, he pushed back to the surface and pulled in her leg, then her torso and finally flipped her around so that her face was above water.

People had gathered on the shore. Some helpers had built a chain linking their arms together until they were able to grab them.

Back on the bank, Nepomuk rolled Enya onto her back and found that she was looking at him but didn't move.

"What were you thinking?" he spluttered.

"Am I dead?" she asked.

"Yes, yes you are!" He was furious. What a stupid question.

Unmoved, she got up and pushed through the crowd watching them and walked back to the bakery.

"Why do you even care about me?" she flung around as soon as he entered the shop after her.

"I don't know. Maybe because you were the first person who stayed with me after Humphrey left."

He remembered how happy Humphrey was when he found him, and that the promise to stay with him was so powerful that the old man had overcome his fears and prejudice to cross the river. As much as this place could be a land of plenty, facing eternity alone was the greatest punishment even if you had everything.

Enya still glowered at him.

"I wish I didn't care, but I do. You remind me of my daughter. But I know that I am not your father and, to be frank, I don't want to be, because you can be quite a handful. I still care for you, and it hurts to see you repeating the same mistakes."

"I didn't try to kill myself," she finally whispered. "I know I'm already dead."

Nepomuk couldn't help but roll his eyes at this admission.

"I just didn't want to be here anymore with no chance, not even death, to get away from it all."

This was a hard admission for Nepomuk to digest and he was lost for words. Who knew that paradise and hell could be the same place?

"Why did you get this ugly extension?" Enya suddenly asked and walked to check out the greenhouse, leaving wet footprints on the floor.

"I didn't. Tthe knitters and weavers had a meeting here, long story," he explained.

"You mean to tell me that's what a bunch of lovely elderly ladies get up to in their spare time?"

"Well, they checked out some men, people, everyone with a skill. See? That's where all of this came from."

Nepomuk pointed at the pile of robust and filigree art pieces, which Enya inspected sternly.

"Did you know that the kids came up with a sweetie that included the toothpaste? And made toothbrushes out of edible gummies?"

"Really?"

"Yeah, and they actually work."

"That makes me feel even older. I've been trying all day to come up with new bread creations, but I'm just too old and dusty to come up with anything inspired."

"Some things just don't need to be made better. They are good the way they are no matter how old. And that counts for inanimate as well as for animate objects."

She smiled at him apologetically.

"Do you know if the river is safe to swim in? I feel like my skin is crawling with ants," she said as she made a bucket to tip out the rest of the water from her shoes and wring out her jumper.

"I don't know. I think it was supposedly this river that Achilles was dipped into as a baby and that made him invulnerable, apart from his heel," Nepomuk explained.

"Well, that's not much use after you've died."

For the rest of the day, or at least the next few hours, they tried to decorate the greenhouse extension to make it more homely. They hung up drapes, created café tables and used the chairs that were now amassed in the shop. Should Georgina claim them back, they would have to make new ones, but for now, the mismatched furniture went well with the disarray of the shop.

The cuckoo clock struck eight and Enya noted that it was off.

Nepomuk wondered whether it was even worth setting the clock. It seemed that in the last twelve hours that the belltower had tracked, Enya had experienced an entire week or two. What was the point of having clocks if time still stretched differently for different people? But then again, maybe you could fit a month into an hour simply by being active and making new experiences.

"Wouldn't it be nice to have some plants in the corner?" suggested Enya as they appreciated their efforts.

"It would. That reminds me, how did you make those sunflowers?" asked Nepomuk.

"I stuck some seeds into the ground and watered them," said Enya.

"Nothing else?"

"That's it. Why?"

"Because it seems like no one else has made any plants and I don't think the creation of life is granted to the deceased."

"I really don't know. What does Achilles say?"

"Achilles? I don't think he ever ... wait, Asphodel fields, the fields of death."

"Sounds pretty accurate."

"No, asphodel is also a plant with white blossoms, which means that there must have been flowers here at some point. Persephone ate pomegranate in the underworld, and Heracles stole Hades' three-headed dog and its spit turned into wolfsbane."

"Wolfsbane? I think you might have taken some illicit drugs."

"No, I just remember my school lessons on Greek mythology. The question still remains why no one has made any plants yet?"

"Maybe they don't care about plants."

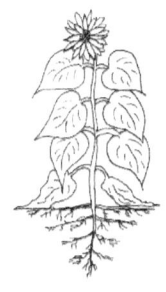

Chapter 13

NEPOMUK COULDN'T BELIEVE that no one cared for plants. Plants were the epitome of nature back in the living world and he associated nature with life. Just because they were dead didn't mean they couldn't strive for life around them. They also made a place so much more homely. He created several flowerpots, filled them with soil and pushed small stones in it before watering two orange trees, ferns, and some asphodel. He and Enya placed the pots around the greenhouse; after all, it was constructed as the perfect environment for plants.

"What do we do now?" asked Enya.

"Whatever we want," said Nepomuk.

"I don't know. It feels like nothing really has a purpose here."

"Does it need to have a purpose? You can do everything you've always wanted to do. Open a shop with weird but wonderful things, pretend you are Wonder Woman and fly around, create fashion."

"Create fashion? Really?"

"Well, or write a book."

"For what? No one needs to make money, and everyone can make whatever they want."

"But some people are better at making certain things than others."

"And why would I be good at writing a book?"

"I don't know. You don't have to, just take your time to find what you enjoy. But it can't be worse than this."

Nepomuk fetched the book he'd created and showed it to her. To his surprise, she sat down and started reading it.

After he had cleared the shop enough to put the bread onto the shelves, he began baking again, since Enya was still engrossed in his book. He wondered whether she could read, since in his opinion it was just gobbledegook.

He was halfway through his load of baking when he heard the doorbell and Enya had left again. He hurried out to see where she had gone and saw her walking into the little café next door. He stayed outside to see whether she was coming back out or whether this was a secret entrance to the underbelly of the underworld.

The longer she was gone, the more anxious he grew. Finally, he walked in his apron over to the café. He saw Enya chatting with the barista through the window and scurried away before she saw him.

At the corner, he made out the community noticeboard and decided to have a look. He still hadn't given up on digging up those drug dens, or at least get someone else to do the dirty work. As he had thought, there was an advertisement for the knitters and weavers with contact details for Georgina. He quickly pocketed the little cutaway with her details and was just opening the door to his bakery when Enya came back with two mugs of coffee.

"Were you watching me?" she asked as she saw him.

"No, I just needed some fresh air."

She eyed him suspiciously. "Here, I got you some coffee. You know, now with the indoor seating, offering hot beverages would be nice."

She went inside and sat back down at a table, flipping open the book and warming her hands on the mug.

"How long did it take for your sunflowers to grow?" asked Nepomuk as he inspected the flowerpots.

"Not long; maybe a few minutes. But it could have been longer, you know, with time being so funny here."

Neither the orange trees nor the fern had sprouted, but when he looked closer at the asphodel, he saw tiny mounds of soil and underneath were little green heads.

Nepomuk finished his baking. When he came back out, Enya was still sitting there reading. The asphodel had now grown into a decent little sprout and Nepomuk watered them again.

"It's funny that only certain plants seem to grow here," he muttered.

"Maybe it's only ones from mythology?" Enya suggested.

"I don't think sunflowers were ever mentioned."

"That doesn't mean they didn't exist back then. Why are you so obsessed with plants anyway?"

"I'm not; I'm just curious. Maybe that's something you should be more, too."

"My curiosity has only ever gotten me into trouble. And you know, so far, you have only done exactly what you knew from your life. How to make bread. Why don't you do something new?"

Nepomuk was taken aback but didn't want to get into another fight.

"You know, you are right. I always wanted to learn the violin. I'll go and get one."

Nepomuk left the shop without another word. It was true, he had always wanted to learn to play the violin, but his main purpose now was to find Georgina and tell her about the dangerous morass that was developing under their feet.

He walked along the river and picked up small stones, which he turned between his fingers for a while before dropping or throwing them away again. With every stone he imagined he was holding an asphodel seed that he was sowing into the barren land.

At the sixth street, which ran vertical to the river, he entered the city and then walked one block further. Pleasantly surprised, he noticed street signs and house numbers. This street was called Weaver Road, and on the corner to Knitters Avenue he found a small corner shop not dissimilar in style to his bakery announcing the Spinners' Heaven in gold letters. It appeared that the flat right above it also belonged to the shop as it was built in the same style, with a bay window and wooden shutters. Next to it on Weaver Road was a massage parlour with blacked-out windows and on Knitters Avenue was a kindergarten where Nepomuk could see children clapping and singing along to loud music, their squeals of joy reverberating onto the street. Above the flat was a gym where every spin cycle in the window was occupied. For some people exercise just for the sake of exercising seemed the height of freedom even in the afterlife.

He could see why a woman like Georgina got frustrated with the uncontrolled construction and occupation of buildings. When she started her shop, this must have looked like a pleasant location in suburbia. Instead of simply moving her shop after the city expanded, Georgina must have made it her destiny to regulate people's desire for settlement and self-fulfilment.

The shop was closed. Even after he had knocked several times, no one opened the door. Maybe she was out for a coffee, although Nepomuk couldn't picture her sitting relaxing in a café somewhere. He decided to walk around a little. Maybe he would bump into her on one of her errands.

The city had grown again considerably since the last time he visited it and in some places he wasn't sure whether he could see the sky anymore. Cars were not only on the road but also in the air and he felt threatened by their shadows flitting along. Despite the growth, he also saw many more derelict shops, and when he walked around a corner to the amusement park, the top levels of a high-rise dropped two floors as they disintegrated into dust. Astonishingly, the building remained intact; apart from the screams of the occupants, to whom this must have felt like an earthquake, and the shower of dirt that came down from above, nothing else happened.

When he arrived at the amusement park, he realized that he had been walking around with a purpose. If he couldn't find Georgina, he could at least investigate for himself what was going on in this area.

The rides were still running on high speed, but it was noticeable that fewer children were sitting in the carts, flying saucers, or riding on dragons and butterflies. Nepomuk found a stall that sold those toothpaste and toothbrush sweets and was truly amazed at how well they worked.

"This is fantastic. Did you come up with these?" he asked the girl who filled the shelves by seemingly conducting to the Christmas music.

"No, my friend Lin made them, but she's gone now."

"Gone? Where?"

"I don't know. She just wanted to go home," said the girl. "I think I might go soon as well."

"But why? Isn't this every child's dream? No parents, no bedtime, as many sweets as you like?"

"Were you ever a child?"

"Of course I was."

"And after a long day at school or even at the playground, didn't you just simply want to snuggle? Be held and taken care of?"

Nepomuk nodded as he thought back to his own childhood.

"There is no place for us to go to just feel safe. It's not always just about fun and games."

"But there are kindergartens. I saw one a few blocks that way."

"Yeah, that helps a little. But they open and close again all over the place. Somehow, no one wants to take on the responsibility of looking after us forever. In the end, there is just no replacement for home, you know?"

Nepomuk knew all too well what she meant.

"And are there any adults here at the park who might help you?" asked Nepomuk innocently.

"Nah, the only ones that come here either just want to have fun like us for a little while or those weirdos coming out of there every now and then. We stay away, because very few people seem to come back out."

The girl pointed at an unassuming brown door on the other side of the street. Just then, a flying taxi landed – or rather, hovered over another car as there was no space on the street – and released a group of three who scurried to the door and disappeared into a dark corridor beyond.

Nepomuk thanked the girl and made his way across the street, which was not that easy as the traffic seemed particularly busy here. He made a mental note to tell Georgina that zebra crossings, traffic lights or maybe even bridges would be useful and thought at the same time how the tables had turned and how glad he was not to be the mayor anymore.

He wondered how many people were still here who remembered the fantastical battle between Knight Lukas and Danilo.

The door turned out to be locked, just like Georgina's shop. He knocked and knocked but no one opened. Maybe he needed a password or a secret combination of beats. He tried several rhythms. At the last one – he wasn't even sure what it had been – the door swung open.

A heavy bass beat vibrated in the walls and Nepomuk felt his way along as the corridor became increasingly darker. When the door closed behind him, his eyes could make out a faint red light at the end of the corridor and he almost fell when he reached the top of a flight of stairs. Now he could make out human noises from down below, and he hesitantly followed them.

Behind several heavy black curtains and a zigzag of walls, he finally entered the underground clubs. At first, he saw nothing much unexpected. Several bars were arranged in circles with different coloured drinks held in long glass tubes that almost looked like the windpipes of a church organ.

People bustled around, chatting, drinking, kissing, but everything seemed fairly innocent. All around this room, which turned out to be round, hung more black curtains that seemed to lead to other parts of this underground party village.

Nepomuk tried to imagine himself at an age where he would have enjoyed such a place to not draw too much attention and walked with purpose across to another curtain.

The room behind was filled with people raving to the sounds of a live DJ. Nepomuk passed along the wall when someone fell into his arms and began touching him almost as if they were controlled remotely. The eyes that looked at him seemed hungry, with pupils that barely left any room for the colour around them.

He freed himself from the arms, which somehow seemed to multiply, and stumbled backwards through another curtain. Breathless, he turned around only to find a mass debauchery of naked bodies. Though at first sight the participants seemed to be enjoying themselves, there were also bodies that seemed to be lifeless and others trying to crawl away only to be pulled back into the pile of arms, breasts, legs and heads.

Nepomuk turned and tried to go back where he came from, but the black curtain was not behind him anymore. He had to pass through the room and almost sprinted to avoid being grabbed by the tentaculous arms.

Through the next curtain was a quieter room filled with blue reflections and people floating paralyzed but wide-eyed in bubbles.

"Where is the exit?" Nepomuk asked someone dressed up as a mermaid, who was operating a human-size bubble machine.

"Why do you want to leave?" asked the mermaid sweetly, as she injected a blue liquid into the arm of a customer before trapping him in a bubble.

"I don't think there is anything here that I like."

"Have you tried anything?"

"No."

"Then how do you know?"

It was frightening how much this conversation reminded Nepomuk of himself trying to get his son Marek to eat a green vegetable.

"I don't want to."

The mermaid looked him over and turned to her next customer without another word.

He tried another curtain and found himself in the dungeon that Enya had talked about. People in cages, on leashes, or strapped to walls with their limbs spread out and others who would inflict pain on them.

Nepomuk closed his eyes and held back the urge to throw up. *I want to get out of here; I want to find the exit.* He repeated this thought over and over again. Without opening his eyes, he felt around until he found a curtain. When he stepped through it, he was back at the stairs that led him up and outside.

Breathing in the fresh air, he leaned against the wall next to the brown door to shake off all that he'd seen.

After about fifteen minutes, he walked further along the street, scrutinizing the few people who were also on foot. Where were they all heading?

Most people jumped straight into cars or, by the sounds of it, into helicopters on the tops of buildings. Quite frequently, there were garage doors in upper-level walls and once Nepomuk observed a garage door opening and a car flying straight out. Despite the thousands of people who must have been in the underground clubs, it still seemed that many more just led a normal life, or at least normal in regard to the possibilities of this place.

As there was barely any footfall, most shops on the ground floor had closed or were purely workshops with a note to call for custom-made items and delivery options.

Quite suddenly, this depressive scenery changed into an airy wide mall with some elaborate knitted sunshades strung from one side of the street to the other. Despite not shading from any sun, their intricate patterns and at times joyful colours brightened this place, and Nepomuk recognized the cloud café, which seemed to still be going strong.

Not far away, Nepomuk saw the ladies from the knitters and weavers club making a team effort to fasten yet another knitted sunshade to a wall. As Georgina was shouting out commands from the safety of the ground, four ladies held the bottom of a ladder whilst poor Marge was stretching at a dizzying height to secure the fabric to a hook under a window.

"Why didn't you ask to get access to that apartment up there?" asked Nepomuk as he positioned himself next to Georgina.

"Why? Because no one was home, of course," she answered the apparently stupid question.

"It looks very nice," said Nepomuk trying to soothe her.

"It does, doesn't it? It gives this whole area a put-together and tucked-in feeling."

"Are you planning on doing this in all streets?"

"We have all eternity," she whistled.

"And how is your guild selection coming along?"

"Ach, don't remind me of that. People are so antisocial, no one wants to have any responsibility even though everyone wants only the best of the best. Entitled beyond their last breaths."

"So, you have given up?"

"I'm not you. I will never give up."

"In that case, may I bring some urgent matters to your attention?"

She scrutinized him quietly. "Consultation hours are between three and five on Mondays and Thursdays. There is a suggestion box at our Spinners' Heaven headquarters, which is emptied every day before noon, but due to the oodles of inquiries, we are already two weeks behind viewing all of them."

"I see. I must say that is a very well organized and sane approach. I will write a letter about the criminal activities occurring in the underground clubs near the amusement park. I'll make sure to mention that their entrance is through a brown door and that drug dealers are luring the children of this city into their dens. But no worries, I will also pop around during one of your consultation times."

Georgina stared at Nepomuk and completely forgot to shout orders to Marge.

"I think the shade should be pulled a little tighter; it's sagging compared to the others," said Nepomuk and nodded as a farewell.

"Wait. Are you saying people are now making drugs?"

"Oh yes, but as with everything, not everyone is good at it, and some people take advantage of the poor souls trapped in their devious net."

"This is outrageous! Why would people do that if they can have everything they want and live without a sorrow in the world?"

"I think it's exactly that. Most things become rather mundane if they become available at the blink of an eye. Maybe when you are dead, other things become more important."

"Like drugs?" Georgina shrieked.

"Like emotional experiences."

"But you don't need drugs for that!"

"You are right, I'm just afraid people might be overcompensating and are not just satisfied with holding hands."

"Are you saying they are doing other things as well?"

"I'm pretty sure they do and not always with the consent of everyone involved."

"Consent ... involved ... not," Georgina was speechless for the first time. "I thank you for bringing this issue to my attention. Marge! Come down, we have more important things to discuss!"

Nepomuk was surprised but satisfied that he had finally found a way to talk to Georgina and lead her in a specific direction rather than running head on into a wall.

"Do you still want me to put my concerns in writing?" asked Nepomuk, enjoying his upper hand.

"That won't be necessary. A brown door, you said?"

"Yes, opposite the amusement park, two blocks down."

"Marge! Come down. Now. There is crime in this city that needs to be taken care of."

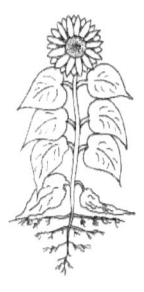

Chapter 14

NEPOMUK WANDERED IN A zigzag path back to the river. Fortunately, or maybe unfortunately, he had been right. Establishments that offered interpersonal connections in all their colours were booming whilst all the little creative boutique shops receded into the grey abandonment of past times.

The frightening thing was that any relationship formed without deeply caring for the other person was doomed to spiral into neglect and misuse and could trap unfortunate souls just like any potent drug.

Back on the shore, Nepomuk discovered a new bookshop, The Happy Ever After, next to his bakery. He was glad to see that despite the spreading decay in the city, there were still people who followed their dreams and let them become reality.

He found his bakery empty but for the bread that he had made, and that Enya must have sorted onto the shelves of the shop. Enya, however, was nowhere to be seen.

Worried about her, he went back out and looked up and down the shore until he saw her coming out of the bookshop with a pile of books in her arms. A woman followed her, carrying another pile.

"Hey, did you find a violin?" asked Enya when she saw him.

"No, unfortunately there are no instrument makers in town," he answered, eyeing the book titles, which ranged from *The Great Gatsby* to *Wuthering Heights, Of Mice and Men* and *Les Misérables.*

"Rather depressing reading," he commented.

"On the contrary," chirped the women behind Enya. If this was the shopkeeper, she couldn't have read much if she didn't know the content of the books. That, or she had a rather dark sense of humour.

Nepomuk held the door open and followed both inside.

"Maybe you could put a note on the noticeboard?" suggested Enya.

"For a violin?"

"Yes."

"Good idea."

"Thank you so much for your help," said Enya to the woman.

"My pleasure. And if you need any more books, just come back. There are hundreds and thousands of stories that need exploring."

"I will," said Enya as she settled into her corner of the greenhouse, surrounded by the blooming pots of asphodel and her books.

"You must be the aesthete who came up with this very unique pirate-space adventure," she said on her way out.

"I might have been," he said, uncertainly.

"Oh, Nepomuk, this is Mireille. Mireille, this is Nepomuk," introduced Enya.

"I like your style. You don't need to be so modest about it. Maybe we can work on some projects together," Mireille smiled brightly.

"Maybe."

"And bring your violin. I like men who are musical."

"I need to learn to play it first."

She left him with a pleasant laugh.

"I think she likes you," grinned Enya.

"Of course she does. What's not to like," he said and turned the sign on the door to 'open'.

As before, the deceased came in, decided on one or more of Nepomuk's delectables, asked a few questions and left. Some sat down to eat an eclair or a slice of his bread-base cheesecake, which turned out to be very popular, or had a hot beverage. He had followed Enya's suggestion and created a simple coffee machine that even he could operate. It didn't take long before the shelves were empty again.

Enya stayed in her seat and read one book after another, only changing the leg she sat on every so often.

"Here," said Nepomuk when he brought her a croissant and a hot chocolate. "What are you reading now?"

"*Romeo and Juliet*," said Enya, showing him the cover.

"Not the happiest of plays," he said, worrying how these tragedies might impact her mental state.

"On the contrary. Mireille has rewritten all the books in her shop to have happy endings."

"Oh." Nepomuk finally twigged what Mireille had meant earlier. "Well, I'll leave you to it. Let me know if you need anything else."

Nepomuk baked more bread and Enya read more books. The shop opened and closed and Nepomuk kept watching the young woman who slowly seemed to shake off her past life. He knew she was changing, changing her mind, changing what she wanted to do, changing her future, and with every book that got put down after its last page, he was more certain that she would leave.

The last book she read was not a tragedy. Nepomuk didn't notice when she finished it, but as he turned around after filling the shelves with fresh rolls, Enya was watching him.

"Finished them all?" he asked with a smile.

"Yes."

"I'm sure Mireille has more," suggested Nepomuk hopefully.

"I'm sure she does, but I think I'm done for a while."

"Would you like a hot chocolate?"

"Yes, please."

Nepomuk made two cups and sat down with her.

"*The Last of the Fianna*," Nepomuk read the title of her last book out loud. "Never heard of it."

"It's about a boy who is brought to Tír na nÓg, the Land of Youth, by a magical horse, where he meets Oisin, the hero of the Fianna. My grandma gave it to me. It was pretty much the only book I ever read." She wiped a tear from her cheek but smiled.

"I think I have to go," she finally said.

"I know."

They sat in silence amongst the asphodel plants, drinking their hot chocolates.

"I'll be right back," Enya said when she placed her empty cup down.

"Where are you going?" asked Nepomuk, fearing that she would just abandon him to avoid a long goodbye.

"I'll be back, I promise," she said and squeezed his arm.

Nepomuk opened and closed his shop and still Enya was gone, but just as he finished sweeping the floor, the doorbell rang and there she was again with a black case in her hand.

"Where did you go?" asked Nepomuk, relieved.

"Sorry, it took longer than I expected. The city is a real dump," she explained, rolling her eyes. "Had to walk for miles to find any shop that wasn't a seedy backroom casino or a brothel. Here."

She popped the case open and carefully removed a brand-new violin.

"The guy said it plays as well as a Stradivarius. Seemed to be quite proud of that."

Nepomuk took the violin and turned it in his hands.

"You've got no excuse now," Enya laughed.

"You could stay and hear me practise," joked Nepomuk.

"Tempting. Very tempting," smiled Enya.

"Thank you so much. I won't disappoint you, although how would you know if you're not here anymore." He waited for a response, but Enya only smiled. "When will you go?"

"Now. I don't trust that I will ever go otherwise. As sad as it is, this city is not the best place for me to be. Maybe I'll find Tír na nÓg."

"I'd make you a magical horse to take you, but sadly I cannot."

Nepomuk paused, reluctant to let her go, but then opened the door for her.

"I'm glad I met you. This kinda made up for my shitty life," said Enya.

"Thank you for keeping company with an old geezer like me for a while."

"You're not old; you are in your best years."

Enya stopped at her sunflowers, which were ripe with seeds and had already started to wither. Maybe they knew that she was leaving, or maybe this was just the circle of life.

She peeled a handful of seeds from the flower's disk and put them in her pocket.

"You never know. I think I will plant some more wherever I settle. They brought me luck arriving here."

Nepomuk smiled, but then had a revelation.

"Did you bring the seeds with you?"

"I had them in my pocket when I died. Peeled them off a slice of stale bread that I meant to have for dinner. It's like a habit whenever I get sunflower bread."

"I think that's the secret," laughed Nepomuk.

"What? Eat the bread while you are still alive?"

"No. You brought the seeds with you. That's where they came from. You can't create life here, but you can bring it with you."

"So, if I had a dog in my pocket, I could have had a dog here?"

"Maybe not. The dog would have to die too, I guess."

"Shame. By the way, where are all the animals anyway? Is there a special pet heaven? That's what I always imagined."

"I don't know."

As elated as he had felt when he thought he had figured out the secret about how to create plants, he felt downtrodden after all the open questions that he could not answer.

They walked side by side along the river to the point where they had said goodbye to Danilo.

"A magical horse would surely be a great help," Enya sighed as she looked over the never-ending plain. "Forgot to put that in my pocket. Actually," she suddenly said and began drawing a bicycle into the sand, "they say you never forget how to ride a bike. Let's see."

She held an elegant lady's bike with a basket on the handlebar.

"Wait a moment," Nepomuk said and raced back to the bakery.

As quick as the wind but panting like a steam train, he came back with a fruit loaf, a jar with a quarter of Herman, and a checked cloth, just like Danilo had made for his journey.

"Here, just in case. When you feel lonely you can eat a bit and remember me."

"Is that the one for your wife?"

"Yes, but I can always make more."

He wrapped the bread and the jar in the cloth and placed it in the bike basket.

"Until we meet again," said Enya, and pushed off.

The bike rattled over the stones; it was lucky that she had made a sturdy frame.

"Now I know why they call it a deadly treadly!" he heard her shout as she steered to the smoother ground near the river.

On his way back, he was intercepted by Mireille. She was apparently running out of space inside her shop as she was busy filling bookshelves outside.

"Bonjour, monsieur!" she called as he passed.

"Hello. Mireille, isn't it?" Nepomuk asked as if he wasn't quite sure.

"Well remembered. If you have a moment, I think I might have a book you'd be interested in."

Reluctantly, Nepomuk followed her inside.

"Maybe an expansion is in order. I know someone who is very good at making greenhouses," said Nepomuk conversationally.

"Oh no, I just want to give people the chance to get their favourite books even when I'm closed. And a greenhouse is really not the best environment for books. The pages would yellow, and moisture is the death for my precious darlings."

"You know a lot about books," commented Nepomuk.

The bookshop was actually right after Nepomuk's fancy. Of course, it had shelves full of books, but it also had nooks with armchairs, a decorative fireplace, and even a spiral staircase to a second storey that was, too, filled with books. The books themselves were bound in dark green or red and had golden or silver lettering. This classy appearance stood in stark contrast to the titles that Nepomuk read in passing. They appeared to be classics, but for the type of book that usually would have a kitsch painting of a man and a woman in a state of half undress.

"Here, I'm sure you've read it already as I found elements of it in your book, but I made some subtle changes that elevate the story. In my opinion, of course," she said with a chuckle, and handed him *Treasure Island*. "I know artists are either crippled with self-doubt or have an inflated ego. I must confess, I belong more to the second class, but at least this should count for something, you know? Self-awareness is an important character trait. In my opinion. Anyway, take it. I would be honoured to hear your thoughts. Maybe you won't even notice my changes; as I said, they are very subtle."

"I'll do my best," said Nepomuk, faking a smile. "But I've also just gotten a violin and want to learn it, thoroughly."

"Oh, so you did find one?"

"Enya found it. And I promised her that I would study very hard."

"Such a nice young lady. Is she your daughter?"

"Um, no. I hope my daughter is still very much alive."

"Of course, of course," Mireille said, placing a comforting hand on his arm. "I know how you feel; I had a daughter. Although we weren't on the best of terms when, you know, when the reaper knocked on my door."

"So sorry to hear."

"She was – *is* – such a wonderful person. Very clever and talented. She studied biology, even got a PhD, you know, Doctor of Philosophy.

"I'd like to meet her, if it weren't for the circumstances," Nepomuk replied, trying to find an excuse to leave.

"You'd like her. She can be a bit headstrong at times, but who isn't. She got that from her father."

"I should really get going; my customers are waiting," said Nepomuk finally.

"Oh, sure. And let me know how you're going with the book. And your violin practice. I personally always liked some Beethoven or Mozart myself, you know, *A Little Serenade.* Maybe you can serenade me one day," she giggled. "But only if you want to," she added seriously.

"I'll see how I go."

Nepomuk was sure she said something else, but he had quickly closed the door and waved at her non-committally through the window.

At his bakery, the first thing he noticed were Enya's sunflowers again. They looked really dreadful now and Nepomuk decided that it was their creator's absence that made them wither. He harvested the seeds and wondered who had first brought asphodel seeds to the underworld.

A handful of the seeds went straight back into the soil, and the rest filled a small bowl that Nepomuk took inside to make sunflower bread. Mireille's reimagination of *Treasure Island* went straight under the counter.

Somehow Enya's decision to move on made him feel strangely lightheaded and empty. This vacuum slowly filled with new baked creations that resembled farm animals, flowers, and plants. He used the sunflower seeds to give them eyes, scales, horns, or leaves, and even though their ingredients and preparation were not new, they looked very special. The smell that came from the oven when he baked them was wonderful and Nepomuk could not resist eating a goldfish while it was still hot. The taste was even better than the smell; Nepomuk wondered whether it was the fresh and real sunflower seeds when otherwise everything else was created from dust.

He also made a new batch of fruit loaves. For the first time, he started to doubt whether it was the right decision to wait here for Blanka. There was no hesitation in his heart that he should try and find her when she arrived, but whether he had to wait exactly here was the question.

What if he moved on like the dead seemed to be destined to do? What if there was a real Paradise or the Elysian Fields rather than this mirage that he had founded? He was torn between staying and leaving. He made a deal with himself that he would stay as long as it took him to learn the violin.

He opened the black case and took the instrument out. How difficult could it be? He had built an entire bakery from his imagination and saw a little boy defeat a grown man in armour. The bow strings needed tightening, but he quickly figured out how to turn the knob at the end. Nepomuk thought that he was off to a good start.

The chinrest felt like it was made for him, the neck of the instrument lay readily in his hand and his fingers pressed lightly on the strings. Carefully, he placed the bow on the A-string and imagined a doleful melody he had heard growing up but didn't know the name of.

The bow screeched along the string like nails on a blackboard. Nepomuk tried it again with the other strings, but to the same effect.

After some more trial and error, he found that the bow hair needed even more tension to make the strings sing. Finally, he produced a half-decent note, but the bow kept on bobbing along the string like Enya on her bicycle.

The smell of overdone fruit loaf interrupted his new ambition. Frustrated by this interruption as well by as the rough start, he packed the violin back in its case and opened his shop instead.

His animal creations were a success; the ones where he added a red jam or tomato filling that oozed out when you cut into the baked bodies were particularly admired. He wasn't sure whether this was an appreciation of realism or just a gory fetish that dead people might be fond of.

Nonetheless, he made his next creations even more realistic and included skeletons that gave a nice crunch. Whilst he was waiting for a dough to rise or a batch to brown, he kept at his violin practice, but after maybe ten cycles of a week's worth of work, he decided that he might need a music teacher, at least for the basics.

As he had no desire to walk through the city again, which was looming more and more menacingly behind his little shop, he placed an advertisement on the noticeboard.

Not many ads were posted on the boards these days, and he had a quick glance through them. Someone was offering oriental carpets, another lifelike replicas of people's pets, and Mireille had hung up a poster for her bookshop.

He read her slogan: 'A happy ever after is never too late, and what better time to get one when you're already dead.'

Someone else was just posting an ad.

'Looking for: 24h security guard. Offering: anything hand-knitted (socks, jumpers, blankets, long johns, cosies, oven mitts, mittens, lampshades, sunshades, sofa cushions, sofa covers, wigs, hats, and dolls). Social company included.'

"Georgina?" Nepomuk said when he looked at the old woman next to him.

Chapter 15

GEORGINA LOOKED AT HIM with clouded eyes. She was old, positively ancient, and suddenly Nepomuk thought that maybe she had had the right to treat everyone else like a child compared to herself.

"Mister Mayor," she responded with a wispy voice. "Didn't think I would see you again."

"Why not? Aren't we all here for all eternity?"

"Not all. People are leaving. They don't want to put up with the mob in this town anymore."

"So, you have not managed to drain the underground swamp behind the brown door?"

"Brown door, red door, black door. Pretty much everywhere you turn now is filled with filth. The cancer has grown too big and I'm afraid it is inoperable now. Everyone is chasing this emotional gratification you spoke about, whether gambling for useless treasures or getting tortured for pleasure. The worst are the gangs that only find pleasure in dominating others."

"Is that why you are looking for a security guard?"

"Yes, though I'm afraid it will be a fruitless quest. Everyone decent has already left. Only Marge and I are still holding the fort."

"Why don't you come to my bakery for a hot beverage and a slice of cake and relax for a while," Nepomuk suggested.

"If it wasn't so already, this place would be my death," Georgina said as they walked to his bakery.

Despite her shrivelled exterior, she still had some spring in her step.

"I always thought I was a good person. I know I can be somewhat overbearing at times and maybe harsh, but it's only ever for the good of other people. Surely I did not deserve a place in hell?"

"I don't think this is hell," said Nepomuk.

"Well, it's not paradise, let me tell you that. Have you been downtown recently? If ever something had an underbelly, it's this town. And I blame you for it." She stopped to point a finger at him.

"Me?"

"Yes, you. Wasn't it your bakery that started it all?"

Nepomuk did not know what to say. After a short awkward pause, Georgina walked on only to stop again to look up at the bookshop.

"I don't know why you were so lucky to get decent neighbours whilst I'm being punished with either a childcare facility or an adult wellness establishment. If ever a book were written about it, you would go down as the godfather of pandemonium, the founder of Sodom and Gomorrah, the—"

She didn't get to continue her little tirade as Mireille had come out of her shop, eager to join them.

"I think a history book about our town sounds superb," interrupted Mireille.

"And who are you?" snapped Georgina.

"Oh, I'm sorry, I am Mireille Dupont, the owner of this bookshop, and I would love to volunteer for this project."

"What project?"

"Writing a book about the history of this city."

"Well, there is not much to it. Nepomuk here, the godfather of pandemonium, built a bakery and all hell broke loose."

"I'm sure there is more to tell."

They had reached the bakery. Nepomuk wondered whether it would be too strange if he took a walk around the block right now, but Georgina just walked right in without waiting for him to open the door.

"Of course there is, like the little boy who made a knight fly like a chicken."

Mireille looked flabbergasted, but Georgina didn't care to elaborate.

"If this one is the founder of Sodom and Gomorrah, that little boy was the architect of the devil's playground. Never in my life have I seen such a hazardous amusement park as that child's dream."

"There is an amusement park in the city?"

"Yes, where have you been? Under a rock?"

Nepomuk had quietly proceeded to make hot chocolates all around but started to feel sorry for Mireille. These two women were polar opposites, but he was sure which one would win in a mental battle of backhanded compliments and open insults.

"Georgina, remember, this place is only as good as its inhabitants, and I would say you are one of the most prominent figures here," Nepomuk said, trying to rein in Georgina's bad mood.

"That's right. I should be standing above it all. I apologize," Georgina said royally.

"That's alright. And you are right. I haven't been around town yet. I get so much from my books that I don't need very much else," said Mireille.

"So, you like books and you write yourself?" Georgina clearly tried to make polite conversation.

"Oh yes, well I like books. I was a librarian. I haven't actually written my own books. I just dabbled here and there in creative writing."

"How fascinating."

Nepomuk shot a reprimanding look to Georgina when he placed her hot chocolate in front of her, and she surprisingly shut up.

"Yes, even when I was young, I was already a real book worm. Always loved them."

"Was it because your own life wasn't ideal?"

Nepomuk threw her another scolding look, but Georgina shrugged to say that she was 'simply making conversation'.

"Oh no, I had a lovely life. I grew up on the coast and I spent my summers catching crabs and my winters ice skating. But of course, finding hidden treasure or travelling to long lost times was not possible except for my books."

"And I bet one or more steamy romances; only literally, of course."

"I must admit, yes."

Georgina pursed her lips trying not to openly show her derisive smile.

"I guess that's why you picked that name for your bookshop?"

"Yes, isn't it clever? I mean you really only get a happy ever after when you find each other here in the afterlife, where everything is for eternity."

"Well, I guess life has this one snag that it ends when you die."

"Exactly." Mireille positively beamed that someone seemingly understood her.

"I assume you are recreating all the books from memory. As a librarian, you must have a pretty good working knowledge of all the great literature."

"Yes, with my own little additions or creative freedom, as I would call it. By the way, Nepomuk, how did you like *Treasure Island*? It's been so long since we last saw each other."

"I've been really busy," Nepomuk apologized.

"So, you haven't even started?" asked Mireille, disappointed.

"So sorry. But I did start practising my violin."

"I was hoping to get some feedback. As I said, I only ever did a little creative writing and was eager to hear whether I am moving in the right direction."

"I can tell you that Enya devoured all the books you gave her, so I am sure you have some talent," said Nepomuk.

Mireille's face lit up. "Well, promise me you'll read it soon."

"Cross my heart and hope to die," said Nepomuk.

"Well, that's a promise never made then," mumbled Georgina under a cough.

"Would you like a pastry with your hot chocolate?" asked Nepomuk as a diversion, but Mireille didn't seem to have heard Georgina anyway.

"Yes, please," said both women in unison.

He served them a small pig and a cow on the Chinese tea plates.

"You made these?" asked Mireille admiringly.

"Aren't these my plates?" asked Georgina.

"Yes, and yes. You never picked anything up, so I put them to good use."

"I guess that was my own fault. Though you could have tried delivering them," grumbled Georgina.

"I only followed what you told me."

"Why is everyone suddenly following what I say?"

Georgina cut the pig's head off and stared unfazed at the red filling pouring out from its neck. She then expertly spun the pig on its back and made a long cut along its belly, flipped what would have been the skin to either side and inspected the crunchy skeleton inside.

"That is rather impressive," she finally judged. "Were you ever inspected and approved as a baker?"

"Not that I know of," admitted Nepomuk.

"I thought as much. That scoundrel didn't seem to be good for anything. But Marge liked him; she has a penchant for troublesome fellas. There's a story for you," she said to Mireille, who had dribbled some jam on her blouse trying to eat her cow with her hands from the bottom up.

"How would you like to become Guild Master of the Bakers?" Georgina asked.

"I think I'll gratefully decline that honour."

"Can't hold it against you," said Georgina and stabbed the pig's leg with her fork and disjoined it at the hip. "This is rather delicious. Well done. I also like what you did with this eyesore of an extension. You almost don't notice that you're sitting in a greenhouse like a monkey in a zoo."

"I thought you liked the extension. If I'm not mistaken you called my shop outdated and that it would be unfortunate if I removed the greenhouse," said Nepomuk.

"True, I do find your shop outdated, but I hoped that you would get in touch with that builder I recommended to get rid of the monkey house and change it into a matching extension. Now, let's hear you play the violin. I always liked live music with afternoon tea."

"Oh, I don't think you want to hear that," said Nepomuk, ashamed.

"Come on, don't worry. No one is born a master and I've heard plenty of bad music in my life."

"No, really. I can't even play a scale yet."

" *Yet* is a good word when learning anything new. I promise I won't criticize you."

"Oh please, I would also love to hear you play," begged Mireille as well. "I can turn around if you like. I always did that when I had to recite poems in class."

"You mean you spoke to a wall?" asked Georgina incredulously.

"Yes. I would always get so nervous seeing everyone looking at me."

"But the other pupils still saw you."

"Of course, but I couldn't see that."

"I see. In that case, turn around, please." Georgina shook her head as Mireille turned to face the curtain.

"Right, we are ready. But don't expect me to look somewhere else."

Nepomuk gave up, fetched his violin, and got in position.

"Do you leave the tension on your bow when you pack it away?" asked Georgina.

"Yes."

"Don't do that. Tighten to play, loosen to put away. You'll thank me when your bow lasts for longer."

"Okay. I didn't know that."

"Go ahead." Georgina checked that Mireille was still facing the curtain.

Nepomuk placed the violin under his chin and expected another interruption from Georgina, but she only watched him expressionlessly.

He pulled the bow along the first string and found that it sounded quite nice. As Georgina was still watching him, he continued to also bow the other strings.

"Any finger work?"

"No. I told you I'm not very good."

For the first time, Nepomuk saw Georgina genuinely smile at him, then she got up and corrected his posture.

"Stand up straight and shoulders down," she said and pushed two fingers into his back. "Rest your violin lightly on your collarbone and your jaw gently on the chin rest. Now, support the neck with your hand as if you're holding the head of a baby. A baby I said, not restraining a snake. Loosen up. That's it. The main points are between the base of your index finger and your thumb. Strike again but this time keep the bow perpendicular to the string and parallel to the bridge."

Nepomuk hesitated.

"Go on, nice *legato* strokes, up and down. I know we have all eternity, but I still don't want to waste a single minute."

Nepomuk did what he was told and was amazed how clear and consistent the note sounded and how effortlessly he could hold the violin.

Georgina indicated he should keep on playing. For the next ten minutes or so, he did nothing but bowing one string after the other.

"That was already very good. I want you to practise this whenever you can. Get a feel for your instrument. Listen how the harmonies change when you play *sul ponticello* or *sul tasto*, that is, when you place your bow closer to the bridge or the fingerboard," Georgina instructed.

"Have you been a music teacher, if you don't mind me asking?" said Nepomuk when he released the instrument.

"I don't mind at all. I have been many things in my life. Once I was a concert violinist with the New York Philharmonic Orchestra. I played in Carnegie Hall under John Barbirolli and was the youngest player to make the cut."

Nepomuk stared at her in awe.

"Close your mouth or the flies will get in."

"Could you play something for me?"

Despite some hesitation, Georgina took the violin from him.

"This one is well made," she said.

"Enya got it for me. Said it was supposed to be close to a Stradivarius."

Georgina raised her eyebrows and seemed quite keen to play.

With great care, she tucked the instrument between her chin and collarbone, placed the bow on the string, her hand held elegantly like a ballet dancer, and then began to play.

She got lost in the music and while she was playing, she looked like the twenty-year-old who had performed at Carnegie Hall, and when she ended it almost felt like the light dimmed.

Mireille awoke with a snort as she almost slid down her chair.

"Wonderful, absolutely wonderful," Mireille applauded into the curtain. "Nepomuk, you are a natural," she said when she finally turned back around.

"Keep it up, and I'll show you how to read music and do the finger work next time I see you," said Georgina. "And remember: Tighten to play, loosen to put away."

She watched him relax the bow hair and tuck in the precious instrument.

"When will we meet again?" asked Nepomuk avidly.

"I do have some other things to do. Keeping Marge on the right track and trying to keep this place from ruin. But make some more of those pastry animals and you'll see me soon enough."

"I can't wait," said Nepomuk honestly.

"And please invite me, too. I had such a wonderful time," piped Mireille.

"She likes you. My condolences," whispered Georgina on her way out.

"Is it just me or didn't she look that old anymore?" asked Mireille, who was still sitting on her chair. "I could almost imagine that she was good-looking when she was younger."

"I think she was stunning," said Nepomuk.

Mireille eyed him suspiciously.

"It's this place," he explained. "Many people change how they look depending on the memories that are currently the most present. That boy Danilo even managed to look older than any memory he could have had of himself. It was rather disturbing. But, you know, with the right amount of imagination, nothing is impossible here. Or at least almost. If you don't mind, I really need to start baking again. Wouldn't want to disappoint my customers."

"Oh, of course, you do what you have to do."

Mireille still showed no sign of leaving, so Nepomuk left her where she was.

Uplifted from the mesmerizing music, he created intricate cakes, filled appetizers, and even brushed up on his skills to make marzipan decorations with gold detail worthy of any Vienna coffeehouse, and he did not forget to feed Herman and make a fresh batch of fruit loaves. He was relieved to find that Mireille was gone when he came into the shop for a short break.

He had ten minutes between batches and decided to practise his up and down strokes.

By the time he opened his shop, he felt quite confident in his posture and the sounds he enticed from his violin. He even experimented placing the bow higher or lower on the sides and found that the closer he got to the bridge, the hoarser and ghostlier the sounds became, whilst moving closer to the fingerboard resulted in fuller and rounder, almost romantic, notes.

Mireille turned up halfway through his opening time but sat quietly with a book where Enya had sat and ate a slice of cherry Danish that she managed to dribble over her top again. She also looked different somehow, but Nepomuk couldn't quite put a finger on it.

Georgina did not turn up and Nepomuk was rather disappointed, even doubting himself. Maybe she had managed to hide her derision for once and had only politely said that he was fairly good.

Chapter 16

MIREILLE HAD MADE IT a habit to come whenever his shop was open and sit and read, occasionally dripping some cake or sauce down herself, but there was still no sign of Georgina.

When he had closed his shop for the third time, and after he had made sure that Mireille had disappeared inside her bookshop, he stepped outside to have a look up and down the river, hoping he would spot Georgina somewhere. Whilst he did not see the old woman, he saw that his asphodel seeds, which he had spread last time, had taken on quite well and formed pleasant patches of green and white on the dry soil. His sunflowers had also grown up again and formed plump buds that could open any moment.

The flowers were not the only thing that had changed, and Nepomuk wondered whether he should go out more often. Just as the blossoms had grown, the city had fallen and looked like the hollow teeth of a once majestic but cruel monster. All but a few of the high-rises had collapsed, and smoke or dust clouds hung over the remaining cavities. Cars stood abandoned in the middle of the streets, and the few people he could spot in the distance hurried along as if being chased by demons. What a contrast to the shops on the riverside, which still created a picture of harmony, although only a few remained here as well.

Nepomuk didn't mind; it meant that Blanka was more likely to spot his bakery, which was still glinting in pink and turquoise.

He had grown tired of practising his up-and-down strokes, but when he tried to play a scale it sounded awfully out of tune. Frustrated and pig-headed, he put the violin away and vowed not to touch it again until Georgina turned up. However, this also meant that he had to find a new occupation to pass the time besides baking.

He stood lost in the middle of his shop, wondering what he was doing here, and he had to remind himself that he was waiting for his wife. He looked around and remembered the book that Mireille had given him. Reluctantly, he retrieved the book from underneath the counter. For a short moment, he considered sitting down in the greenhouse, but decided against it, as he didn't want Mireille to find him. So, he went to the small chamber behind the oven he had originally made as a bedroom, but had never used so far.

The bed was comfortable, with a soft mattress and a thick eiderdown duvet. He turned on the bedside lamp, which gave the room a warm shimmer, and wondered whether he should make himself a nightgown before getting into bed. In the end though, he only took off his pants and shirt as he would have hated for sand to get between the sheets.

He crawled under the duvet just in his underpants and vest and opened the first page.

The book started authentic to the original version describing the Admiral Benbow Inn where the boy Jim Hawkins met the sailor Billy Bones. But then it started to deviate. A couple of old mates came to visit Billy Bones and they had a lovely time drinking in the Inn, before leaving with heartfelt goodbyes. Then Billy Bones gave Jim Hawkins a map to Captain

Flint's pirate treasure and told him that he was too old to re-
trieve it, but if Jim managed to find the treasure, he could keep
it if he promised that the old sailor could stay at the Inn until
the end of his days.

So far so good. Mireille had removed all the violence from
the book and the worst thing that happened was that Jim promised to keep the old sailor without asking his mother first.

The book then briefly returned to its original plot, where
Jim managed to convince the local physician Doctor Livesey
and Squire John Trelawny, who conveniently owned a ship, to
fit out an expedition. The crew, however, did not turn out to
be permeated by former pirates and the cook Long John Silver
was a very jolly fella with a knack for putting on feast after feast
with only barrels full of apples at his disposal. The feasts were
described in minute detail, making up the pages that would
have been filled with mutiny and violence. They reached the
island unharmed, a few kilos heavier and the best of friends,
to build a fort to live in whilst they scoured the island for the
treasure and to fill up Long John Silver's pantry with coconuts
so that he could keep on feeding them on their way back.

Needless to say, they all returned in the best of health, di-
vided the treasure fair and square, and lived happily ever after.

Nepomuk read the book in one sitting, though he admittedly skipped about half the pages where food, trees, sand, water, or any other inanimate object was described at length.
Why in the world, and indeed the underworld, did Mireille
think he would enjoy this version of the book? Maybe it was
because Long John Silver also turned out to be an excellent
baker.

After this disappointment, he was still curious enough to
look through the books that Enya had devoured. Every one of
them felt thinner than he remembered. Some of them could

be reclassified as short stories; a regular women's weekly magazine could have printed them whole. And due to their adjusted contents, they would have been quite suitable for such a format.

Of Mice and Men had been boiled down to a goofy buddy road trip with never-ending descriptions of the beautiful Californian landscape. *Les Misérables* became a romantic love story set in 1950s Paris. The only tragic moment came when Fantine died only to reappear again, explaining that she had faked her death for some unknown reason. The only text where he accepted that the changes led to a more enjoyable read was *Romeo and Juliet*. Mireille had included only minor changes, which improved it by not improving it, and made sure that Romeo did get the letter explaining the ploy. They lived happily ever after in Mantua, though no one knew what they did for the rest of their lives.

He wasn't sure what to do with the books. He had no desire to read any more of them but was also against throwing books away. Returning them to Mireille was a possibility, but she would surely want to know whether he had read them all. If he denied this, she would just insist on him taking them back with the risk of giving him even more.

In the end, he decided to build a bookshelf and have a little library where his customers could pick a book and hopefully never return it.

Mireille was delighted when she saw his arrangement and called it 'ingenious'. She herself was the first to pick a book and sat in her usual spot to re-read *The Comedy of Hamlet*. Nepomuk swore he heard her sigh in glee and at times even chuckle.

Everything went as usual until it didn't. A man and a woman ordered some of Nepomuk's animal pastries and stayed at the counter to eat them. They were tittering obtrusively and waved their animal heads around on their forks like an executed person's head on a spike.

"Could you maybe not do that in here?" asked Nepomuk as politely as possible.

"Why? Don't like us playing with food?" asked the woman.

"No, it's the kind of game you are playing."

"Shouldn't have made food that looks like animals then," said the man, oinking with his pig head in Nepomuk's direction.

"Please, finish your meal and leave," suggested Nepomuk.

He never had to deal with this type of behaviour and felt his heart rate increasing as he rattled through his options in his head.

He could try to demand some respect by building himself up in front of them, though he had never had a particularly impressive figure. Maybe crunching his knuckles? If he managed to imagine himself as a strongman, he could grab them by the neck and throw them out.

A young boy asked for a slice of Christmas roll and as Nepomuk prepared it, one of the troublemakers stuffed his whole pig head into his mouth and let the red filling dribble down his chin like a bloodthirsty murderer. The boy ran out before Nepomuk could do anything.

"That's enough. Please leave, now," said Nepomuk in the most authoritarian voice that he could muster, as he felt his knees becoming wobbly.

"Alright, alright, we'll leave."

"Really?"

"But only if you sell this for us, and by *selling* I mean sprinkle it on your cakes. You know, easy as taking candy from a baby, or givin', if you know what I mean."

The man secretively pushed a small bag with white powder over the counter and tapped his nose like a sleuth.

Before Nepomuk could do anything, the two of them were grabbed by the ear and a very angry Georgina, looking as though she could have been in a woman's wrestling team, pulled them howling and cursing outside.

"I told you to clear off the last time I met you. This is what happens to people who don't listen."

Georgina berated the two troublemakers and then grabbed an umbrella from a passer-by to spank them until they were running to save their skins.

Everyone was craning their necks to watch this spectacle and Mireille was dripping clotted cream and jam from her scone that hung mid-air in front of her mouth.

"Watch out for those nogoodniks. Now that the town is crumbling because no one with a right mind is left to imagine a better place, they come out of their holes like rats," warned Georgina when she came back inside, still holding the umbrella.

"What do you mean, no one is left?" asked Nepomuk.

"I said no one *in their right mind*," corrected Georgina.

"You are still here," quipped Mireille and garnered a deadly look.

"Only just. I have come to seek shelter," she said and Nepomuk could see a glimmer of fear in her eyes. "I do not admit this lightly, but I have failed."

"Don't be too harsh on yourself."

"It's like casting pearls before swine, and this is a whole pigsty full. Marge has left, everyone's left, just those lowlifes keep hanging about hoping to find others to torture. I've already taken a step back and accepted that there might be lost souls who like it, but when they try to force their perverted minds on others, that's where I draw the line. Reluctantly, I've met my Waterloo."

"Surely you don't mean actual torture," asked Mireille, wide-eyed.

"Torture, torment, ordeal, call it what you want, but people hurt each other, and not like in a heartbreak romance novel."

Mireille looked shocked.

"I think it's good you are not going out much. You wouldn't survive long."

Mireille looked deeply hurt.

"Have you changed your hair? You look younger?" asked Georgina, apparently not quite unaware that she had also caused emotional pain.

"Oh, just a little bit," blushed Mireille.

That's what she had changed. By now, it must have been a couple of decades that she had slowly taken off her appearance.

"Anyway, do you have a little spot for me? I'll be as quiet as a church mouse," asked Georgina.

"Of course. I have a second bedroom that I made for Enya. She never used it."

Mireille looked envious about Nepomuk's offer.

"I'm not surprised. She looked like a troublemaker herself," judged Georgina.

"She probably was, but if you catch people in the right moment, even the worst can be saved. The problem is usually that these moments are short and rare," said Nepomuk.

"Well said," applauded Mireille.

"Where is she now?" asked Georgina, probably expecting that she was degenerating in some drug den.

"She escaped before she couldn't anymore."

Georgina nodded silently.

"Right, as payment for my lodging, you will learn the violin. Did you practise your bowing?"

"Yes," said Nepomuk, too eager to continue with the music lessons to take offence from her phrasing.

He closed the shop, unpacked the violin and was just getting into position when Georgina interrupted him.

"Before we start, hot chocolate and that last piece of marzipan cake to get me over my shock."

Nepomuk hurried to get everything to her, but before he could pick up his instrument, Mireille asked sweetly whether she could also have a refill and he trotted back behind the counter.

When both women were finally served, he proudly demonstrated the four dulcet sounds he could produce on the violin. Georgina asked him to keep playing *sul ponticello* and *sul tasto,* as well as trying to more abruptly change his up and down strokes and the angle at which he held the bow to the bridge.

"This already sounds mesmerizing," said Mireille, with her chin placed in her hand. "I love musical men."

Georgina rolled her eyes and finished her cake and drink when the bow began to bounce off the string and Nepomuk feared he had done something wrong. But Georgina wiped her mouth and announced that he was doing some quite nice ricocheting there.

"I think it's time for you to learn some actual notes."

She pulled a sheet of paper out of her bag that she had obviously handwritten. It contained five horizontal lines with letters written on each line as well as black dots with vertical lines attached.

Mireille got up and peeked over his shoulder. "This almost looks like an enigma code for a treasure."

"Don't be ridiculous. The Enigma used a polyalphabetic substitute cipher to encrypt a message written in morse code. This is just a musical alphabet."

Nepomuk wondered whether Georgina was at one point in her life involved in the secret service but didn't have time to ask.

"There are seven notes to a scale, and unlike on a guitar there are no markings on a violin that tell you where to put your fingers. I's say that's the only encryption. I will give you a little help but hitting the right notes has a lot to do with muscle memory."

Georgina took the violin from him and produced some slim silver tape from her bag. She positioned the violin between her legs and began to pluck the strings whilst pressing down on them with her other hand. When she had found the right note, she placed a piece of the silver tape around the neck.

"There. These indicate where to place your fingers for the first position. Have a look at that chart. I want you to practise day and night until you can do it in your sleep."

She demonstrated how to play a simple C-scale and then passed him the instrument.

The next half an hour, Nepomuk played, and Georgina corrected him, either hands on or with verbal cues. When she started to write more cryptic music charts, Nepomuk felt good about himself, as he thought this was a sign that he was doing well.

Nepomuk played the C-scale on different strings for so long that his fingertips started to hurt.

"You'll have calluses there in no time," said Georgina when she saw him looking at his fingers. "I think that is enough for now though. Never play until you're bleeding. That is anything but romantic."

Mireille had fallen asleep again.

"You wonder what exhausting things she is always up to that she needs to sleep that much," commented Georgina.

"Maybe she gets really involved in the stories of her books."

Chapter 17

THEY QUICKLY FOUND A great rhythm; Georgina tidied the shop and wrote études for Nepomuk to practise while Nepomuk baked and played the violin.

Mireille read book after book and Nepomuk's little library did the opposite of what he had intended, as it grew with each book she finished until he had the feeling that she had also moved in with him.

When Nepomuk had a firm grasp of the basics and his fingers remembered instinctively where to hit the strings, the pieces that Georgina gave him grew more complicated, requiring more time to practise, and Mireille offered to take on the customers when the shop was open.

He played pieces that no living ears had ever heard as Georgina secretly fulfilled one of her lifelong dreams, which was to compose.

As the music rang out from the little bakery by the River Styx, the city crumbled and returned to the dust it was made from. There were no cars, no coffee shops, no casinos, or drug dens left, and the people had moved on. First the righteous, then the lost souls, then the vampires who had fed on both.

Nepomuk had just mastered Massenet's *Meditation* and finished the final contemplative notes when he opened his eyes and saw Georgina cry in silence.

He watched her and knew that she had been moved by his playing; something that he had previously thought impossible.

"Not an Itzhak Perlman, but good," she finally said. "I have one last piece for you before I go."

"But you can't go. There is still so much I need to learn. See, my back hurts; there must be something wrong with my posture."

"Nonsense. Stop eating all that cake and lose the belly weight and it will sort itself out."

"I'm with Nepomuk: we have found a nice little rhythm, almost like a family," said Mireille. "Mother, father and – what's the opposite of a grandchild?"

"There is no such thing," snapped Georgina. "I taught you everything I know. Now it is up to you to keep it up, feel the music and make it your own. That is something no one can teach you. Here." She showed him the pages she had been working on since she had moved in. "I'll play it once for you and then you do whatever you want with it. I call it *Music of a Lifetime.*"

She took the instrument, gave it a quick tune, and began. The music started like a joyful child's play only to change into the heavy and complicated notes of adulthood akin to Bach and Mozart. As she played the forlorn music of a wife who had lost her husband during the war, Nepomuk heard the thunder of the crumbling loop-de-loop in the distance, and when she played the soft romantic notes of finding love after death, Nepomuk looked at Mireille, who was sitting again with her head in her hand and her elbow in the crumbs on her empty plate.

A short interlude told them about her second marriage, the children she had had, and the travels she took before finishing with the aching melodies of a long farewell.

"The curse of a long life," Georgina said when she ended. "I vowed never to be the last to leave again, and I think it is high time for me now."

Without a word, Nepomuk went back and fetched a fruit loaf, which by now had become more of a token for farewell than the bread of love he had always thought it was.

"Here: I know you don't need it, but it might make your journey easier," said Nepomuk.

"Com pani. Sharing bread. I am glad as much as I am surprised to call you my companion in this hereafter. I'd even venture to call you a friend."

"I don't think I have ever received a greater honour."

For the first and last time they embraced each other and Nepomuk felt deep emotions welling up inside him.

Both Mireille and he moved to accompany Georgina outside, but she stopped them.

"Stay. I don't need your soggy faces to watch me. I hope you find what you are waiting for, or rather that you'll be found. But don't waste your time. Cheer up and get practising."

Nepomuk mustered a smile, and then the doorbell rang, and Georgina was gone.

"I can see now why you like her, or even love her," said Mireille, resigned.

"What? I don't love her."

"Maybe not," she sulked. "But you like her more than me."

She laboriously made her way around the tables and to the door.

Nepomuk was torn. It wasn't that he didn't like her, he just felt indifferent towards her. He didn't want to get her hopes up but also didn't want to hurt her anymore. By the time he had sorted through his feelings, Mireille had paused for a long while with her hand on the door handle, then finally opened it and left.

The shop was very quiet all of a sudden. As he stood and listened, he realized that it wasn't just his shop. He peered through his window and saw the dead arriving as usual, but the noise of the city had completely vanished now, and no one stopped to look around anymore.

He stepped outside and confirmed that only Mireille's bookshop and his bakery were left, and both had started to look run-down and flaky around the edges. Only his sunflowers stood in full bloom and the asphodel had spread over the plain that was once the city.

Mireille was talking to some deceased and handed out armfuls of books. When she saw that he was watching her, she disappeared inside.

Nepomuk also went back inside to bake some more bread but then plucked up the courage to walk over.

No customers were inside the bookshop, and it didn't look as though Mireille had had many visitors at all as the shelves and books had accumulated a thin layer of dust. Suddenly, a couple of books came flying down and almost hit him on the head.

"Hey!" he shouted out in surprise.

"Oh, I'm terribly sorry, I didn't think there was anyone else in here," sounded Mireille's voice from the open gallery. "Oh, it's you," she added when she saw him.

"I came to apologize."

"For what?"

"I don't really know, but I seem to have upset you."

She climbed down the spiral staircase with more books in her arms.

"You don't have to apologize. It's the story of my life. Unloved and unwanted, even by my own family."

"I don't think that is true."

Nepomuk didn't get an answer. "Look, I like you ..."

"You do?"

"Just not in a way that you might want. I think I never told you why I am here. I'm waiting for my wife."

"Oh, I didn't know you were still married. No ring." She pointed at his left hand.

"I rarely wore it. It didn't comply with the hygiene standards, you know, as a baker handling food items with my hands."

"I see. And you really think you can find her? I mean, has anyone ever met someone that they knew again?"

"Not many, but I know of one. The main reason though is that very few people wait."

"But you do." Mireille sat down in an armchair by the fireplace.

"I read your book," Nepomuk said, trying to cheer her up.

"Really?"

"Yes."

"And? Did you like it?" Nepomuk waited a little too long. "You didn't."

"It wasn't the worst I have ever read." That was true, as her version of *Les Misérables* was much worse. "I just think you might have lost some of the things that made the book exciting."

"What? Like blood and thunder?"

"Yes. Taking people on a journey that they would never experience in their own lives."

"But I want them to experience a wholesome story. Look at what happened to this city. I know I have no first-hand experience, but wasn't it the bloodlust, the cruel fantasies, the addiction to pain that was its downfall?"

"Yes and no. I think those bad emotions are just a part of human nature, as are good emotions. The question is whether we can regulate them, whether there are any rules that teach us how to control them. Unfortunately, this place has no, or very few, rules to obey and some people got lost. The good people quickly moved on and this city seemed to be like a filter where all the dirt got stuck."

"But still, we don't need to fuel their bad behaviour by giving them bad examples."

"But all these stories are not just rule books about how to be bad, but about the suffering and injustice that can happen to people, often at the hands of others and due to no fault of their own. They hold up a mirror for us to recognize the bad and to allow us to do the good, the righteous things."

Mireille sat quietly.

Somewhere above them the rafters creaked, and a cloud of dust came down on them.

"But why can't people just learn the good without the bad?" Mireille asked.

"I don't know. I guess you could have sunshine without shadows as long as there was nothing to cast them. But as soon as you put humans in the picture, there are bound to be shadows. That doesn't mean they are bad. Sometimes too much of a good thing can be just as unpleasant."

Something struck a chord and Mireille looked up at him sharply.

"My daughter used to say that. All my life, I've been trying to be good to people, to help where I could. I thought my husband loved me, but I think he only needed a lot of help, and when he finally found his own feet, he got up and left me. Said

I was too needy. *I* was, after I had given up twenty years of my life to make sure our family would survive. Same with my mother: she had one child after another and I, as the eldest daughter, had to help her raise them from the moment I could walk. And I did it for as long as I could. She never forgave me when I left home at sixteen. And my daughter wouldn't even accept any help. No babysitting, no Christmas presents. She said she didn't want to be in my debt. But I never asked for anything in return; just a thank you would have been enough."

A side table with a beautiful Tiffany lamp collapsed and shattered on the floor.

"Nothing I ever built for myself stayed and now even this place is collapsing all around me!" cried Mireille.

"Sometimes, we have to learn to love and value ourselves first, otherwise you might sell yourself short."

"How can helping each other ever be undervalued?"

"Maybe because help isn't always needed. Often people know exactly what they should be doing to achieve something, and they only need a bit of time to figure out how to do it. If someone then comes and does it for them, they will never learn for themselves. They will always depend on other people and might come to resent the dependency."

"So, you are saying I have been the architect of my own misfortune?"

"How about instead of rewriting existing stories, you write your own and find out?" suggested Nepomuk.

"Like a memoir?"

"Yes. And what better place to do it than here, where you remember everything about your life."

"I don't know. I don't think anyone would want to read it."

"You are doing it again."

"What?"

"Thinking about other people before yourself."

"But even I don't think I had an interesting life. Georgina could have written a trilogy; I don't think mine would even amount to a death notice."

"Now, I am making the same mistake that you always seem to. Trying to help someone who doesn't want to be helped," said Nepomuk and got up. "You might surprise yourself, but no one can write your memoir for you."

He walked to the door, which fell from its hinges as soon as he touched the handle.

"Where are you going?" she asked.

"Back to my bakery."

"You are not leaving?"

"Not until I have found my wife again."

Nepomuk baked his entire repertoire but couldn't shake the feeling that he was wasting his time. Maybe Georgina was right. He had a good life but right now he was not achieving anything. He could be making bread for all eternity, but to what end? Feeding the dead? They were never hungry and already dead, so what difference did it make?

Maybe he was selfish to wait for Blanka. Maybe she had found love again and moved on – something that he should probably wish for and be happy about. He never believed in having a one true love, so why not see if he could find a companion here in the afterlife, though not necessarily Mireille. Suddenly, his thoughts took a turn for the worse and he doubted what Blanka had ever seen in him. They had an average life, nothing exciting, no extraordinary achievements or suffering that bonded them. They never lived through war or famine, were never robbed, didn't travel the world, never attempted to change it in any way. And what did he have to offer her now? The same old life, making bread all day long.

Angrily, he slammed the dough on the counter and then threw it with all his might against the wall. As the dough slowly peeled off and eventually fell to the ground, he began sobbing like someone who had lost his last bit of hope.

Desperate for human contact, he went to the only person left, but when he walked out, it looked like a tornado had ripped everything apart. Mireille's bookshop was no more. Instead, he saw her sitting amongst the remnants of hundreds of books in an armchair by the fireplace, which were the only things left.

She was writing furiously on a notepad. Every finished page that she dropped over the side of her chair dissolved like the memories they contained.

She kept on writing until the end. When she looked up and saw Nepomuk, her flushed face was at peace.

Nepomuk knew that this was yet another farewell, the last one, and he signalled her to wait a moment as he went back inside to fetch a loaf of fruit bread.

When he reached her, the armchair and fireplace had also crumbled to the ground, and she stood there as if she were all dressed up with nowhere to go.

"Thank you," she said when he reached her. "I think I understand now a bit more about what was and what wasn't. And I'm sorry if I bothered you."

"You haven't."

"I think I'll move on and see what lies ahead rather than hoping to change what was."

"I figured that much. Here." He passed her the bread.

"Com pani."

"Com pani."

And then she kissed him softly on the lips.

"I hope you find your wife. Please don't give up. I have never heard of a more romantic love story than yours and I would be madly disappointed if it didn't have a happy ending."

Nepomuk smiled. "I won't," he said, even though he had already made up his mind.

"Good. Don't make me come back and rewrite your story. You know I'm terrible at that. If there ever were star-crossed lovers, it is you and your wife."

"I'll take your word for it."

"Good."

They embraced each other, and his last companion left.

Chapter 18

NEPOMUK WAS AS ALONE as he was on the day he had died and arrived on the plains. Or at least, as alone as you could be with hundreds upon hundreds of deceased arriving every minute.

He saw a couple of people peering into his bakery and then moving on, trying to decide which way to go.

The sunflowers were losing their petals and hung their heads heavy with seeds. He filled his pockets with the seeds and decided that this would be the last time he baked bread. Apparently, the shop knew his decision, as the door needed some shoulder-pushing to persuade it open.

The tables and chairs were already a little wobbly and everything appeared wonkier than it used to be. Nepomuk set out to make his last batches of Sunday rolls, sunflower bread, and fruit loaves.

One last time he turned the sign in the door to 'open', even though his shelves were already crumbling away, and the tables and chairs were now unusable.

He gave away bread after bread, roll after roll, answered a few questions about the place, and with each customer entering and leaving, he lost his last bit of hope of ever seeing Blanka again. And then he had only one fruit loaf and some sunflower bread left.

A four-year-old girl in her swimmers and with wet hair was his last customer.

She looked at him with large sad eyes. "I'm cold," she said, and Nepomuk made her a terry cotton towel and a bathrobe.

"Are you hungry?" he asked her when she stopped shivering.

The girl nodded and Nepomuk gave her the fruit loaf.

"Here. It's nice and sweet."

The girl whispered a thank you and a smile flitted over her face before she left.

The doorbell fell off its hook when the door shut for the last time. Nepomuk turned the sign to 'closed' and then went to make his bed and sweep the floors, not quite sure why, but it felt the right thing to do when you left somewhere for a long time.

Then he fed Herman again, wrapped him with the sunflower bread in a red checked cloth, and picked up his violin. Georgina's sheet music fell to the floor and her *Music of a Lifetime* landed at Nepomuk's feet.

He stopped and read the notes that dotted the lines and decided to play it in memory of the companions he had made in the afterlife, but when he began playing, it was not the melody that Georgina had played.

His melody told of the mischief and reprimands of his childhood, his golden and aching times as a journeyman, of the days he met Blanka and his children were born, their pleasant time together and finally the short suffering that concluded his life.

When he opened his eyes again his bakery was gone; only his work counter and the oven with the hook for the oven mitt were left.

He packed away his violin and picked up his travel parcel.

"Excuse me, you don't happen to have any bread left?" someone asked behind him.

"I'm sorry, but I'm all out," he answered as he turned around and saw an old woman.

The woman looked at him as if she had seen a ghost and then sank to her knees.

Nepomuk dropped everything to catch her and as she was lying in his arms and looking into his eyes, she changed into the young woman who had bought the fruit loaf on that sunny day, to the mother who gave birth to his children, to the love who had sat beside his bed when he died. Hot tears ran down his face and he couldn't take his eyes off Blanka.

"Why? How?" stammered Blanka and reached out to touch his face. "Am I not dead?"

"I'm afraid you are," said Nepomuk and kissed her hand.

"But then, what are you doing here?"

"I waited. I waited for you."

"Here? Why didn't you move on?"

"Because I was afraid, I was confused, I didn't know where I was, and I don't know where to go. Not without you." Nepomuk struggled to put his reasons into words.

"But this is such a dreadful place," said Blanka and looked around. "Did you make this?" she asked when she saw the oven and workbench.

"Yes. If you had come a little earlier there would have been our bakery shop."

Blanka looked at him with a questioning smile.

Was he insane? Had he just imagined everything? But here was his workbench and the oven.

"Here, I also made this bread," he added, trying to regain some stability. "I made it from sunflowers I planted."

He handed her the bread, and she took it with some hesitation.

"It smells wonderful," she finally said.

"Try it. I know you don't need to eat, but just try it."

She broke off a corner and then another little bit, which she put into her mouth.

"This is amazing," she said, taking another bite.

"I'm sorry I don't have any fruit loaf for you."

"Why?"

"Because it's your favourite."

"No, it's not. If anything, this is a close contender. I can't think of a better bread I have ever tasted."

"But ..." Nepomuk was dumbfounded, almost heartbroken.

She stopped eating and looked at him full of love. "I always told you it was you and only you that I fell in love with that day."

She stroked his face again. "Why did you stay?"

"I couldn't leave you behind. I'm sorry if that's not what you wanted."

"I wanted to be with you more than anything. But don't you feel this pull to move on?"

Nepomuk didn't know what she was talking about.

"No. If anything, I wanted to go back."

She quietly shook her head. "And you waited twenty years in this solitude?"

"It's been twenty years?"

"Twenty-two, in fact."

"It only felt like a season," said Nepomuk and reminisced about the time. "And I wasn't alone – at least not all the time."

"I'm so glad to hear that."

"Sometimes I even feared I had missed you. But tell me, how have you been? How are Luella and Marek? Did she marry Nicolai?"

Blanka smiled and sat next to him, shoulder to shoulder, watching the river and sharing the bread.

"They are well. Luella and Nicolai married, though we scaled back the wedding and had it with only the closest circle of friends and family. We felt that was more appropriate since you had passed away only recently. Luella was very upset, but Marek gave her away, which was beautiful."

"She should have had a large celebration. A big bash for being alive and in love," Nepomuk burst out.

"But she loved you very much, too."

Nepomuk went quiet again. "I wish I could have been there," he said and both of them had tears in their eyes.

"You have five grandchildren," said Blanka to cheer up the mood.

"Five?"

"Yes, two from Luella and three from Marek."

"Who would have guessed. Tell me."

"Not long after the wedding they had a boy called Michal Nepomuk, after you. And a girl, Jana Karolina. As fate had it, they moved to Australia, which broke my heart a little, but Marek travelled the world and met a nice girl in New Zealand who was from the next village, so they lived really close by. They have two girls and a boy. Such beautiful children. You can be proud."

"And how, how did you ...?"

"How did I die? Peacefully. At home. They all had enough time to come and say goodbye. Marek told me to say *hello* to you and that he misses you."

Nepomuk's heart was full of longing and sadness about the missed years, but Blanka did her best to describe them to him. She told him the funny and the sad events from first words to job losses, from misunderstood words to miscarriages.

"Such a full life," Blanka ended. "I would do it all over again," she said. "With you."

They embraced in a long overdue kiss.

"We might not be able to do it all again, but we can remember everything. Come here," Nepomuk said and lay down.

Blanka looked at him funnily, then moved a couple of larger stones and rested her head on his chest.

"Just imagine you are in a featherbed."

He could feel how she started to relax after a few minutes.

"This is amazing," she exclaimed.

"It's pretty good," he smiled. "And it is so much better now."

Nepomuk held her tight and together they dived into their memories as Blanka caressed his ear with her fingertips.

He didn't know how long they had already been lying there. Nepomuk wouldn't mind if it lasted for all eternity, but Blanka eventually sat up.

"Now I know!" she exclaimed. "You look like the day when Luella started school."

"That was a big day. Our little girl getting out into the big world."

Blanka smirked. "Yet you refused to dress up for it and instead wore your favourite baggy trousers."

"I needed to wear something comfortable because otherwise I would have cried like a baby when she went into her classroom, and we left her there."

"At least now you are wearing the good shirt I gave you for Christmas. We must make for an odd couple, you in your forties and me in my nineties," Blanka said as she looked down on him.

"But you are not. This place allows you to look like the most prominent memory and I'd say you look like that Monday morning when we conceived Marek."

Blanka looked embarrassed, but it was true, and as she slapped his chest and giggled like a lovestruck girl, Nepomuk also changed to look like that strapping mid-thirties baker with muscular arms and flour-greyed hair.

Blanka was in awe at the transformation she witnessed and then they embraced into an even longer kiss. If it hadn't been for the lack of privacy on the riverbank, they would have re-enacted the entire Monday morning.

"You haven't told me what you have been up to the entire time you waited for me. I hope it wasn't too boring," she said when she lay back in his arms again.

"On the contrary."

Nepomuk told her about Humphrey and how the old man had refused to cross the river for decades because of fear of the unknown and how he finally remembered everything when they crossed the river.

He told her about Enya and how he tried to help a lost and broken soul by making sand cakes and how this had led to the discovery of endless possibilities and the foundation of an entire city.

"You can make all of that from nothing?" Blanka sat up to look at the workbench and oven again, which were still standing strong. "You made these?"

"Yes. Look."

Nepomuk scraped some sand together, collected some gravel and sprinkled it on top, pretended to crack some eggs and pour warm milk over it. Then he kneaded the sand, which transformed under his hands into a smooth and elastic dough. He got up to finish his yeast braid on the counter.

Blanka watched with unbelieving eyes.

"And yet, this place looks so barren," she said when he had put the bread into the oven.

"Unfortunately, humans will eventually always create what destroys them. There used to be a café next door, a Wild West saloon, and a bed-and-breakfast – you know, one of those romantic ones that seem only to exist on television."

Nepomuk walked a bit and pointed to where the shops had been; only the asphodel remained now.

"And then it grew into a beast made of concrete and the worst of human nature showed its face. But there were also good people, each in their own way, but kind at the core."

"What is this plant?" asked Blanka and bent down to smell the white blossoms.

"It's asphodel. The Asphodel Meadows were supposed to be where the ordinary people spent their existence after death," explained Nepomuk.

"So, we are ordinary?"

"I guess so."

"And where do the extraordinary go?"

"The Elysian Fields."

"And where are they?"

"I don't know."

Blanka went back to the workbench and the oven, where a lovely smell of fresh bread penetrated the air.

Nepomuk got the yeast braid out with his bare hands as the oven mitt and bread paddle had already disappeared. He balanced the hot loaf on his fingertips and dropped it next to Blanka, who was moving her hand over the worktop.

"What are you making?" asked Nepomuk.

"Nothing," she said.

"I have seen too many people doing this by now," he said suspiciously about her hand movements.

Out of thin air, Blanka created a beautiful glass decanter. Then she clasped the body of the decanter and a moment later, it was filled with a light Pinot Noir infused with the aroma of red berries.

Nepomuk moved his hands and created matching glasses, then Blanka made a blanket and they sat down for a romantic picnic.

"What about that violin case?" Blanka asked as Nepomuk broke the bread.

"You know I always wanted to learn the violin and I had twenty years while I waited for you."

"You must be pretty good then."

"I had a good teacher."

"Go on then, I want to hear."

Nepomuk fetched his violin and quickly looked through the pages that Georgina had written for him to find a suitable piece, but in the end, all he needed was to look at Blanka and the most romantic melody ascended from the instrument.

Blanka watched enchanted.

Nepomuk's heart was about to burst thinking that this was how their time together could be from now on. Romantic picnics by the riverside, serenading her, good food. Blanka had added a selection of cheeses and olives as well as grapes.

"This looks like a feast for the gods," said Nepomuk when he sat down.

They both pulled a face when they tried the cheeses and Blanka admitted that she had no clue how cheese was made.

"I'm sure we'll find someone who can teach you, if you want to learn," said Nepomuk.

"I think I'm starting to like this place," said Blanka. "I can see a nice little house with a cottage garden where I could grow vegetables, and butterflies and bees come to visit my flowers."

"There is one problem," said Nepomuk. "Only plants that the dead have brought over from the living world exist here. And I don't know where animals go after they've died."

Blanka looked disappointed. "So only asphodel grows here?"

"And sunflowers. Here." He pulled out a couple of sunflower seeds from his pocket.

Blanka looked them over. "Did you bring them?"

"No, Enya did."

"If only there was a way to let someone know to bring more."

"I only tried orange trees and fern. Maybe there are other plants that people have already brought over."

"Let's try it. What do I do?"

Nepomuk picked up some small stones. "Here; just imagine the plant you want to grow as best as you can and then scatter the seeds."

Nepomuk threw some grit towards the river.

"What did you plant?" asked Blanka.

"Some grass."

Chapter 19

THEY SAT THROWING STONES around them, imagining fruit trees and berry bushes, oriental flowers and herbs. What grew were apple and pomegranate trees, poppies and narcissus, red anemone and hyacinths. The last stone Nepomuk threw had an oddly three-part structure that reminded him of Hades' three-headed dog, so this stone grew into wolfsbane with its purple blossoms shaped like the hoods of monks.

"These are beautiful," said Blanka and went to pick a bunch.

"Don't touch; it's very poisonous."

Blanka hesitated. "But I'm dead already."

Nonetheless, she did not break the flower and instead wandered around their little meadow surrounded by blooming fruit trees. The oven and workbench in the middle now looked like a sunken fairy tale.

Before long, the trees bore fruit and people began picking apples and pomegranates for their journeys.

"It would have been nice if the grass had grown. How long have we been here now?" asked Blanka. "It only feels like a day, but the trees have had a full summer."

"Time goes quickly for those who are happy and busy, so a day seems about right for us, but for someone else it might have been months or even years."

"It is so beautiful here."

She sat back down and looked him in the eyes.

"How about we build a cottage here?"

Nepomuk felt a strong urge to agree, but he also noticed other people behind the trees who had already begun to create mundane items. He heard the revving of a car, the chitter chatter near a café, but also a loud brawl over an apple.

"Maybe not here," he said.

"Why not?"

"Because nothing good stays that way. I think we should go."

"But where?"

"I don't know; wherever our feet will carry us."

Blanka did not seem convinced and plucked on some wolfsbane that was growing next to their blanket.

"You stayed. And you remained good. Maybe if you are pure at heart everything will stay good."

"I'm sure it will, but it still has to endure the bad that will ensue. Believe me, no one stayed the last time, and it won't be any different this time."

Someone broke through the trees carrying a mobile phone and being followed by a second person.

Blanka jumped up in fear, but the thief and the pursuer pressed on, and they saw them violently crashing to the ground on the opposite side of their meadow.

"I want to stay. Who knows whether we will ever find anything different or better," said Blanka like a sulking child, and her eyes swam in tears. "You can go if you want, but this is Paradise. There won't be anything better."

"What are you talking about? This is not Paradise. This is a mirage at best," said Nepomuk and wondered what had gotten into her.

Then he saw the purple flower in her hands.

"Here," she said and walked to a large apple tree. "This is where our living room could be."

Two comfortable armchairs appeared under the tree.

"And we could have an extra-large bed with comfortable eiderdown pillows and blankets."

A large four-poster materialized in the meadow.

"Blanka, stop it!" shouted Nepomuk. "This is not the place to stay."

At his words, the oven and the workbench collapsed noisily.

"Oh well, we can make a new one," she said, walking hysterically around and creating furniture here and there.

Nepomuk took several large steps towards her and ripped the wolfsbane from her hands.

"But what if I don't want to make bread anymore? This is not it."

She looked at the flower on the ground and then into his pleading eyes.

"We can be whatever we want, just not here."

She slapped him resoundingly across the face, and with the fading sound, the leaves on the trees started to fall.

"I'm so sorry, I don't know what got into me."

"You might not die from it, but something even more dreadful could come over you because of this plant."

Nepomuk began trampling the wolfsbane where he could find it and wondered whether this was one of the drugs that had trapped people in those dungeons.

He needn't have put in so much energy; the plants started to wither as soon as they had made up their minds to move on. Their picnic blanket was merely a checked pattern now on the sand and the decanter dissolved into water that was quickly absorbed into the dry soil.

They packed up the rest of the bread and picked some apples that Nepomuk crammed into his trouser pockets.

"See, I knew these trousers would come in handy, besides being comfortable."

"Which direction do you think we should take?"

"How about inland? Quite frankly, I have had enough of dead people arriving everywhere you look."

And so, they strapped their bundle and started walking.

They walked in silence and Nepomuk knew that Blanka was doubting whether they had made the right decision, just as he had doubts himself. What would they find? Would they find anything, or would it be the same everywhere they went, just maybe with fewer people?

After a while, they heard a thunderous crashing and even felt the earth vibrating. When they turned around, they saw the ruins of what had been a multistorey building, shrouded in dust.

"I hope no one got hurt," Blanka said.

"Not for long, at least not physically, though it can't be pleasant to be trapped under gravel."

They walked on and told each other stories from their lives, but as both remembered everything about their lives, there was very little that they could tell each other that they didn't know already.

One story that Nepomuk hadn't heard was that, at the tender age of ten, Blanka had stolen, or borrowed as she called it, the large cart horse of the smithy in the village where she had grown up. After she had managed to mount it without a saddle or reins, she went for a ride up the hill, or rather the horse took her for a walk. A dark thunderstorm rolled nearer just when the horse had reached the top of the hill, and Blanka had tried to no avail to move the horse back towards its stable. The blacksmith finally found her soaking wet and muddied. Blanka had been afraid she would get scolded, but the smith thought the horse had escaped and she had found it, so he gave her a coin for her effort, with which she bought herself a cheap children's lipstick in bright pink. She never wore it out of fear her mother would see her, and she'd get a scolding for that. This story had been a secret she had taken to her grave, but she was glad she could finally tell someone.

They took a rest and ate a bit more of the sunflower bread. There was nothing around them. No one else had gone in their direction, no other river had sprung up, and the mountains on the horizon remained as distant as ever.

What if Blanka had been right? What if he had made a mistake to leave the riverbank and their little meadow? Nepomuk's thoughts turned dark as they walked on in silence. They had said everything, lived through their memories again and learned a few new things about each other. Nothing ground-breaking that changed anything. He was still in love with her and knew he had made the right decision to wait for her. But had he led them right to their doom, relegated to wander these plains forever? He wasn't even sure if he could find their way back to the river. Theoretically, all they had to do was walk away from the mountains, but just as he could not walk away from the River Styx when he was still on the other side, it appeared that the only way they could go was towards the mountains. If he turned to walk in another direction, the mountains rose higher and higher at the horizon with each step.

They finished the rest of the bread at their second break. If there was anything like distance, Nepomuk thought they must have walked about twenty kilometres by now. Not feeling hungry, nor cold or hot, nor sleepy, he began to feel drained and hopeless nonetheless, and he could see in Blanka's eyes that she was feeling the same.

The stones began to look the same. At one point, Nepomuk walked back fifty metres to check that he wasn't hallucinating and that a larger rock back there in the shape of a sleeping cat was not the same as it was here. He could not tell, which added to his sense of dreadfulness.

"I'm sorry," he said when he returned to Blanka.

"For what?"

"For making you leave a perfectly good place."

"It was neither perfect nor good. You were right: a place without any rules will bring out the worst in people sooner or later. Unfortunately, no one is perfect."

He sat down.

"I don't think I can walk on. I don't want to walk on."

She sat next to him.

"That's okay. The most difficult thing about being dead is probably figuring out what to do and where to go. What's your purpose for the rest of eternity? No-one needs you and in essence, you don't need anyone either."

Blanka took him in her arms, and he cried in her lap. Her words sunk deep inside his heart and with them he disappeared into an ocean of depression. Not everyone could make bread and his little bakery had been well frequented, but it wouldn't have made a difference if it hadn't been there. The whole city, the café on the clouds, the bookshop, even the drug dens and torture dungeons had never made any difference. They were merely distractions for people to stop them from having to face themselves, who they were at the core of their being.

Who was he without his bakery? He was at times mischievous and loved to laugh, mostly with people but sometimes also about people, which was not kind or good but part of who he was. He liked doing things his way and despised people who invaded his private space. He'd rarely tell this to people directly but would rather gossip about them and try to cut them out of his life, which was probably cowardly. He was curious and found that there were many things he had wanted to experience and learn, but he had been too lazy to even attempt any of it. He sometimes envied his neighbours or friends who could afford to go to the theatre once a month and he knew that Blanka would have loved to do that, too, but he was either too tired or they didn't have the money. He might not have committed all seven deadly sins, but he was not an inherently good person. Nor was he inherently bad. He was just average.

"I am so glad to have you," Nepomuk finally said.

"So am I," Blanka said and kissed his forehead. "I think we are very fortunate."

"How?"

"Because everyone else I saw walked on their own. We have each other and I wouldn't wish for anyone else to be here with me."

"Maybe that is what we're supposed to do. Be happy with what we have and everything else will follow."

"Well, I'm very happy."

"Then let's just stay here and create our Paradise."

"Okay."

"Okay."

They both smiled but then Blanka's face looked in wonder into the distance.

"Is that a sunflower?" she asked.

"What? Where?" Nepomuk sat up.

She was right. There, in the middle of this desert stood a single sunflower in full bloom.

"Enya," Nepomuk whispered.

They walked closer. The sunflower appeared to be fresh and full of life. When they reached it, they saw another one in the distance. Almost like a trail, they followed about fifteen sunflowers, and then Nepomuk realized that the mountains that never appeared to get any closer were suddenly behind them.

He didn't notice that they ever crossed them, but he somehow had the suspicion it was not the physical but the emotional path that they had put behind them.

With new hope, they kept walking.

"Look, is that grass?" Blanka asked and pointed to a green bushel that sprouted at the side of a rock.

It was, and in a little while they were walking in a grassy field and all sorts of flowers were springing up around them. Then trees rose in the distance, and they began skipping and running along like little children until they reached a purling little stream. Beyond that stream sat an old man in a white tunic on a rock with a pen and paper.

The man was deep in thought, every now and then scribbling something down before crossing it out again.

"Hello!" Nepomuk finally called. "Can you tell us where we are?"

The man looked up in surprise and quickly hid his paper in a pocket.

"Hello there and welcome. I guess you could call this the Elysian Fields, or Paradise, Nirvana or the Summerlands. Whatever takes your fancy."

Nepomuk and Blanka looked at each other in excitement.

"Where do we go from here?" Nepomuk shouted.

"There is a bridge if you'd like to come over. I can show you around."

Indeed, there was a bridge they hadn't noticed. Nepomuk wondered whether this place also allowed you to make things out of nothing or whether they had simply overlooked it.

"How long did it take you to come here?" asked the man when they crossed the bridge.

"Well, if you don't count the time spent near the River Styx, then I reckon we walked about forty to fifty kilometres."

"Wow, that was fast. Was it torturous, nonetheless?"

Nepomuk was a little taken aback by the gloating yet impressed interest that the man took in their journey.

"It was challenging," he said.

The man nodded and seemed to drift off into his own thoughts.

"Hi, I'm Blanka and this is my husband Nepomuk."

"Oh, of course, how rude of me. I'm Homer."

"As in *The Iliad* and *The Odyssey*?"

"Why, yes," cried the man happily. "It's become rather seldom that people recognize me."

"Really? I thought you were still considered one of the greatest poets that ever lived."

"Why, thank you. It is so nice to hear that I haven't been completely forgotten."

They began walking down a little trodden path away from the river. The nature was so lush and green that it almost felt unreal.

And then Nepomuk saw a bird, or at least he thought that it was a bird as it disappeared as quickly as it had been there.

"So, you are husband and wife, huh?" asked Homer.

"Yes," answered Blanka.

"That's unusual. Did you die together? Was it an accident?"

"No, we died twenty-two years apart."

"Twenty-two ..." Homer stopped on the spot and looked them over. "I don't think I've ever heard of such a case, and I've been here now for ..." He began counting on his fingers. "A very long time."

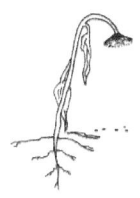

Chapter 20

THEIR PATH WAS SOON lined with cypress trees and Homer led them to a low building made of wood and mud and begged them to enter. After they had crossed a dark corridor, they came into a courtyard with an elaborate channel system that flowed into a beautifully tiled pool in the middle akin to a Roman bath. In the corners stood an olive tree, a fig tree, a quince tree and, oddly enough, a coconut palm.

"Come and rest," said Homer and pointed to a room that was open to the yard and had a low wooden table with stools around it.

Blanka and Nepomuk sat and looked around. To the outside, the house had only small open windows with wooden shutters. Originally ancient Greek, as Nepomuk guessed, the furniture was now a mismatch covering centuries, and strange collectables stood on every shelf and in every corner. Mixed amongst these museum-worthy antiques were the funniest little art pieces made from coconuts.

"I never learned how to cook, but I know how to eat and that is even more important here," Homer said when he returned with several trays laden with fine dishes ranging from smoked fish to creamy goat cheeses, fresh grapes and olives, and finally a whole three-tiered marzipan cake, a tureen with goulash, and an assortment of no less than nine different breads, which Nepomuk found to be exquisite.

"Eat, eat," Homer encouraged them and watched almost hungrily as they tried the cheeses with bread.

"It's very good; much better than yours," said Nepomuk to Blanka.

"Here, have some of the goulash. Harry Houdini gave me the recipe, or rather he made it for me once and I've been copying it ever since. I'm quite fascinated by its taste." Homer poured each of them a bowl. "I still haven't figured out what makes the sweet yet spicy flavour, but who cares as long as it tastes good," he laughed.

"I think it's the paprika," suggested Blanka.

"Is that a fruit?"

"It's a spice made from dried red peppers," explained Blanka.

"Fascinating. Where is it from?"

Blanka looked questioningly to Nepomuk. "I think it's from South America."

"Ah yes. I met a fella once who was from Guatemala. Said that's in South America. I rather like the word. Guatemala. Say it. Guatemala."

"Guatemala," said Nepomuk.

"This is a rather lovely tureen," side-stepped Blanka, turning the porcelain dish around to look at the green and gold images on each side.

"It is. Marie Antoinette made it for me as a gift. She also showed me how to make this marvellous cake."

"You met all these people?"

"Why, yes. Mind you, I don't meet everyone, only if they arrive near my humble abode and I happen to cross their paths. The last guy who stopped here made these for me."

Homer lifted the lid of a silver platter and presented a pile of hamburgers.

"Said this is the cuisine of the 21ˢᵗ century."

Homer watched their faces as they decided on whether to take a hamburger out of politeness.

"Have I not made them right?" asked Homer.

"Oh no, they look exactly like they are supposed to. If you ask me, they probably look even better. It's just, I'm a baker and I know how these types of buns are made, which is not particularly appetizing," said Nepomuk.

"I knew the fella told porkies. Couldn't believe that this is considered good food now; certainly not world class. Anyway, wine? You can never go wrong with wine," said Homer and covered the hamburgers back up.

They were given the most exquisite wine glasses with a honey-coloured grape juice that revived their senses.

Glass in hand, Blanka began walking around the room to look at the displayed items more closely.

"Are all of these presents from people who have passed through here?" ask Blanka as she eyed a curved wooden bow and arrows in a leather sheath.

"Yes; it's a little habit of mine to ask my guests to leave something that represented their life."

"I guess mine would be bread, but I think you already have a very good assortment of that."

"That's true – many people seem to turn to bread making in hard times. Quite funny."

Nepomuk felt a sting and doubted even more that he had achieved anything in his lifetime.

"But making truly good bread that nourishes and tastes good is an art that only few of my visitors mastered. Nine, in fact," Homer said as he looked over the bread varieties on the table. "Mind you, I've been here now for," he counted his fingers again. "A very long time."

Nepomuk felt slightly better. He wondered how easy it would be to make bread and how it would taste here where everything seemed to be full of life. He moved his hand over the table like a magician and there was the most perfect fruit loaf he had ever seen.

"So, you already know how things work here," said Homer, impressed.

"A little. I had twenty-two years to practise whilst I waited for Blanka."

"Were you in that city that the last guy told me about?"

"Probably. I sort of started it, I guess."

Homer nodded, not all that surprised. "It's been a while since the last one."

"What do you mean?"

"Oh, at least once every century someone starts something and that gets the ball rolling and it grows, people follow their dreams and then go overboard until it spirals out of control, and it all comes tumbling down again."

"Always?"

"Always."

"Then how do you manage that this place is still here?"

"I'm not doing anything. I just apply the rules."

At that moment, Blanka stumbled against a fragile table when she stepped backward to look at a ceiling-high painting. The Fabergé egg that was placed on a three-legged stand rocked precariously, and just when it was about to tip over, everything slowed down. Homer got up and casually caught the egg and stabled the table. "You know, I have been here ... a very long time and I think I have a pretty good grasp of what can be done around here."

Everything went back to normal speed, and he set the egg back on its stand.

"I'm so sorry," stammered Blanka.

"No worries," said Homer and looked at the painting. "Rembrandt drew it when he was here last time."

"Wow."

"But we haven't tasted your bread yet."

Homer sat back down and cut half of Nepomuk's bread into pieces.

"This is delicious," Homer said with a full mouth. "Do you mind if I reproduce it every now and then?"

"Of course not. I'm glad it can hold up to your other delicacies. Maybe you'd also be interested in Herman."

"Herman? I didn't see anyone else with you." Homer looked around as if he expected a very small person to be hiding behind Nepomuk's back.

"No, Herman is this sourdough that grows and can be shared with friends," explained Nepomuk as he pulled out the jar with the bubbling mass.

"How fascinating. And what a wonderful idea."

"Keep it if you like. Make bread or pancakes for your guests from it."

"I most certainly will. And what about you? What have you done in your life?" Homer asked Blanka.

"Me? Oh, I've been a mother and the salesperson in our little bakery shop. I'm afraid there isn't much I could offer you."

"She was a fabulous actress," interjected Nepomuk.

"Yes, but that was years; heck, a lifetime ago."

"Doesn't matter. I once had someone demonstrating how he cried as a baby. It was ground-breaking. Go ahead, try it."

Blanka stood quietly, thinking about what she could perform.

"Now I've studied philosophy, and jurisprudence, medicine, and even, alas, theology, from end to end, with labour keen," she suddenly began, and as she acted out Faust's despair and obsession, she walked around Homer's collection, picking items up here and there, and Nepomuk only hoped that she would not break anything.

Then, she moved to the courtyard and looked to the sky and then the water flowing ceaselessly into the pool. "That I may detect the inmost force which binds the world, and guides its course; Its seeds, productive powers I explore, and rummage in empty words no more!" She ended her monologue with her hand stretched into the pool of water.

"Bravo, bravo," said Homer jubilantly as she finished. "Oh, how I love a good story and an even better storyteller."

"Is that a bunny?" Blanka suddenly remarked as she bowed with a glowing face to all four corners.

"Ah yes, they do turn up sometimes and stay a little," explained Homer. "You were brilliant, my dear. Absolutely fantastic. I think I might have something that could interest you. I just need to remember where I put it."

Homer was searching through chests and drawers but couldn't find what he was looking for.

"Ah well, I will find it eventually. I assume you would like to stay the night? It'll be getting dark soon and you are not set up yet."

"There's night-time here?" asked Nepomuk, surprised.

"Yes; I don't sleep too well when it is light."

"Are you making it become night?"

"Yes. You don't have to do it, it's just my rhythm."

"We don't want to intrude," said Blanka.

"Not at all. I'm set up for visitors. I have recently even updated the décor."

Homer led them through the courtyard into another room, which was occupied by a large king-size bed with floating white curtains around it.

"You should find whatever you need in here." Homer pointed to a heavy oak wardrobe. "Just imagine it and you will find it. Here is a wash basin with fresh spring water in the pitcher. My latest addition is this black square, courtesy of the same guy who brought hamburgers to my knowledge. Said it was called a T-Phi, but I haven't figured out what it does yet."

"It's like a theatre where you can watch people act," explained Blanka.

"In here? It's too small for anyone to fit in. I mean, I could imagine it, but really, who would want to see someone squashed to the width of a hand?"

"Here, I'll show you." Blanka turned the television on. "Oh look, it's *The Glass Slipper* with Leslie Caron."

"I still don't see anything," said Homer.

"I see James Bond," laughed Nepomuk. "Shaken, not stirred. It seems we all see what we like best."

"But I still don't see anything," complained Homer. "Ach, I've been here for too long. Missed too many things. Anyway, I'll leave you to it. See you in the morning."

Blanka opened the wardrobe and found an exquisite silk nightdress and cosy pyjamas for Nepomuk.

"You know, I wonder why he still looks so old," said Blanka as she slipped into her night dress.

"Maybe he likes it," said Nepomuk watching her, intrigued. "Being old?"

"What do I know," said Nepomuk and undressed himself. He did not put on his pyjamas but stood there naked.

"What? Don't you like your pyjamas?"

"Not tonight. I quite like how young I look, and I think it's a shame to cover myself up."

Blanka chuckled and with two slow hand movements, she slipped the straps off her shoulders.

They crawled under the blanket and found each other. This truly was Paradise, Nepomuk thought when their lips met.

As Blanka was later lying in his arms, caressing his ear, he could hear the purling of the nearby river and the chirping of crickets before slipping into a dreamless slumber.

Nepomuk woke early; or at least he thought it was still early. A soft rain was falling, and the musty air of wet grass and fertile soil permeated the room. Then the rain stopped, and the sun began shining low through the open window and onto the end of their bed. Here and there he heard a bird sing. All sorts of different melodies, as if a whole chorus of single voices kept on replacing one another.

After they had washed and dressed, they found a lovely breakfast prepared for them. Just like yesterday, Homer kept on serving more and more foods from croissants to baked beans.

"I'm afraid I'll burst if I eat any more," said Blanka, after Homer offered her another slice of apple tart.

"Just imagine you won't," answered Homer.

Blanka lifted an eyebrow and then happily accepted the cake.

"So, what do we do now?" asked Nepomuk.

"Have something more to eat?"

"No, I mean, what do others do? Where is everyone?"

"Well, most people who stay make themselves a home somewhere."

"Anywhere?"

"Anywhere. I think there is a lady from New York just a stone's throw away from your bedroom window."

"Really? I didn't see anything," said Nepomuk.

"She chose not to be seen by anyone."

"I don't understand. No one can see her?"

"Exactly that. You decide if you want to interact with other people. Drives some people nuts if they can't talk to anyone, but others prefer it that way, and here it's all about your own free will."

"So, if I don't want to talk to someone ..."

"Then you simply don't talk to them. But more importantly, if you don't want them to talk to you, they can't do that either. Mind you, they can do the same to you."

"That's crazy."

"Oh, it gets even better. You can be really selective and choose to hear no foul language or insults. That way you can still interact, but everything remains pleasant for you, even if the other person is very rude. Everyone gets their own Paradise."

Nepomuk's head swam. "So, there could be hundreds of people right beside you, but you can't see or hear them?"

He had a sickening feeling imagining that they might not have been alone in their bedroom last night.

"Theoretically, but most people automatically don't allow for invisible people to see them. It's something most people don't imagine happening, so it doesn't unless you explicitly want it to. I've heard of people who do that, but of course only with a two-way agreement."

Nepomuk felt only slightly better, and he could see in Blanka's worried face that she had the same thoughts.

"If you like, I can show you around," suggested Homer. "Keep your mind open, and you will see other people's creations. Close your mind and you will only see what you want to see."

They walked in the direction in which Homer said the lady from New York lived, but the forest only looked thicker in that area. Even though Nepomuk tried to stay open-minded, he could not imagine that anyone lived in that area.

"Good day, Naoko," Homer suddenly called out.

Blanka and Nepomuk followed Homer's wave and saw a slender young man by the river who had slowly moved through a tai chi sequence.

"Homer, how often do I have to tell you not to scare me when I'm exercising," the man called back. "I will block you."

Homer just laughed it off. "These are Blanka and Nepomuk! They just arrived."

Naoko just waved annoyed before focusing again on his exercise.

"He's a very dear friend of mine. Been around for quite some time, too. I think this tai chi might have something to do with how he has lasted this long."

"What do you mean, 'lasted this long'?" asked Nepomuk as they moved along and passed an airy home with open sliding doors, so that they could see right through it. The vegetation had changed, and hundreds of ever-blooming cherry trees surrounded the house. A soft breeze rustled the leaves and blew a cloud of pink petals around them.

"Most people, or should I say souls, move on pretty quickly."

"Move to where?" asked Blanka.

"They reincarnate. To stay here requires that you are fully at peace with yourself. You have nothing left that you need to learn or experience, no apologies left, your self-confidence is in perfect balance. Children usually return pretty quickly to have another go, but I've known some people who have reached that stage and still decided to go back just for the fun of it."

"But why? If this is Paradise, why would anyone return and live again?"

"As I said, this place is not for everyone, and most people figure that out for themselves sooner or later."

They arrived somewhere that looked like an English garden. Sure enough, there was a large manor house set on a perfectly manicured lawn, and on that lawn stood a beautiful brown cow with large horns.

Somehow, the house reminded Nepomuk of someone. Not long after, Knight Lukas stormed out of the house, dressed like a nobleman all in tweed and with a hunting rifle ready to shoot.

"Fuck off, you bloody cow!" Knight Lukas screamed as he stormed across the lawn.

And then he shot.

Blanka clasped her hands over her mouth, but Homer just laughed gleefully.

The cow kept on grazing and even lifted her tail to let go of some impressive droppings. Knight Lukas was now stomping around the animal trying to push it, but the cow didn't even seem to notice him. If anything, it tried to lovingly rub its head on his arm.

"I bet he won't stay much longer. Way too needy that everything has to go his way, but not willing to do his part, despite having reached this place after his path of self-consciousness," said Homer. "Good morning, dear sir. What a fine day."

Knight Lukas stared them down and then turned on his heels to storm back into his house.

"Good morning, Cleo," said Homer gently and patted the cow's head.

Chapter 21

CLEO THE COW LIFTED her head and enjoyed the pet as she ruminated with pleasure.

"So, animals come here as well?" asked Nepomuk.

"Of course. Just most of them go on to be reborn immediately. You see them popping up here and there and then they are gone again. They also don't have to go through that whole cleansing and finding yourself pilgrimage, as they are usually quite well adjusted considering their simple characters."

"That's why there are no animals by the river?"

"Yep. Most babies and very young children reincarnate quickly, too, unless they experienced something dreadful that stuck even with such an innocent life."

"What about this cow then?" asked Blanka.

"Cleopatra, I think, liked being a cow and by now she's been here for so long that I don't think she even remembers that she could reincarnate. And I haven't met anyone who speaks *cow* to let her know."

"When you say Cleopatra, you don't mean ..."

"The Egyptian queen? The very same."

"And she reincarnated as a cow?"

"Yes; you can go back as whatever you want. Some people find it relaxing to take a few rounds as an animal. Shakespeare, for example, is now on his third turn as an earthworm. That reminds me, I have to find the manuscript he wrote when he stayed with me. I really think you would like it," he said to Blanka.

Nepomuk and Blanka were baffled. How could one of the greatest playwrights want to spend an admittedly short life as a worm, and apparently three times in a row?

"And you remember all of the people and their lives?" asked Nepomuk.

"As I said, I don't meet all of them and sometimes I miss a few lives before we cross paths again. They never remember me, just as they don't remember their previous lives, but after a while you recognize some mannerisms or predilections for certain things that are so deeply ingrained that they transpire even between lives. Cleo, for example, always liked men in armour, which is probably why she now sticks around this manor house so persistently. Although she is pretty good at shielding herself from any mistreatment. Plus, she did tell me before she reincarnated that she wanted to see how a cow lived, which also helped me to recognize her again."

A short walk later, they arrived at a small village that was surprisingly lively with a Christmas market on its cobblestoned streets. The sun was setting behind a snow-covered forest and large snowflakes fell softly on the roofs. The scene looked as if it had sprung from an old-fashioned Christmas card sent by a grandmother. Everything, from the twinkling lights to the smell of roasted almonds and glühwein invited you to come in.

"This is one of the few places that has developed where hundreds of likeminded people come together and allow each other in. I quite like it, even though I think they overdo it with the snow sometimes," said Homer.

They wandered in amazement between the little huts and marvelled at the hand-crafted toys and art. Nepomuk even recognized a little mechanical dragon that spit real fire and smiled at the vendor, who did not recognize him but returned the smile.

Homer chatted with people here and there, introduced them or himself to some of them whilst Nepomuk and Blanka ambled hand in hand like new lovers, eating nougat and bratwurst, or warming their hands on a hot cup of cocoa.

"I think I could stay here," Blanka said when they met again on the outskirts.

"Don't make a decision yet," said Homer. "Come."

They followed him away from the village. Strangely, the sun didn't disappear but instead rose higher again until they began to sweat.

The snow gave way to fine sand and the deciduous forest turned into a lush coastline with palm trees and hammocks. Crystal-clear water opened in front of them and even Homer took his shoes off to walk barefoot over the beach, a sunhat suddenly on his head.

"This is one of the few communal beaches where people with a nudist penchant meet," said Homer. "Of course, you can just imagine your own private beach, or mountaintop, or whatever, but I just wanted to show you what is possible."

A group of naked men and women who had enjoyed some drinks at a Tipi bar jogged onto the sand and began playing volleyball.

"This all feels so surreal," said Blanka as she watched the players keenly.

"You'll get used to it. Or not, and then you just move on."

"I still can't see how anyone would move on."

Back in Homer's house, Nepomuk told him more about his time waiting for Blanka and he just nodded along, as if it was an ancient story that had been told many times before.

"These same people, or should I say these same desires and needs that doom every community to fail there still exist here. The only difference is that you can effectively shut out people who try to abuse any sort of power that they think they have over someone else. Very frustrating for them, but very freeing for anyone else," said Homer. "I would have loved to meet that boy, Danilo? He reminded me of Edith Garrud somehow. Can't put my finger on it though. You might have heard of her? No? Part of the suffragette movement, world's first female martial arts teacher, I was told. Anyway. Wouldn't surprise me if he moved right on."

"You don't happen to know who we were in our former lives?" asked Blanka.

"I have a suspicion, simply because you turned up together, but it is my principle not to tell people. For one, I could be wrong, and secondly it tends to go into people's heads and they either flatter themselves or sink into self-doubt."

"So not many people come with their loved one?"

"No, not many at all. But if they do, they usually have a special bond that has already lasted for several lives."

Homer watched them intently. "Ha," he suddenly called and then walked across to their bedroom, where he pulled several loose pages out of the night table. "As usual, closer than you think. Here, this is Shakespeare's last manuscript that he ever wrote as Shakespeare. Thought you might like it. It's a comedy of sorts, though I heard different reactions to it. It's almost a retelling of or sequel to *A Midsummer Night's Dream*, only this time Puck plays pranks on some deceased, making them believe that they are still alive, unnecessarily postponing the realization of their demise. But I won't reveal too much."

That night, Blanka got lost in Shakespeare's last play whilst Nepomuk binged on Indiana Jones. Because she got distracted by his laughter and he wanted company watching the films, they each imagined the other either sleeping or laughing along with them. It was a very enjoyable evening for both.

"How did you like the play?" asked Nepomuk during breakfast.

"I liked it very much, though I thought it was more morbid than funny when Tender tried to kill himself only to find that he was already dead and that there was no escaping," answered Blanka.

"Yes, that's usually the point most people criticize," said Homer. "I find it funny in a tragic way, but what an imagination. I've never met anyone who tried to kill themselves after they were dead already."

"I have," said Nepomuk. "For exactly that reason: she couldn't bear being here and having no way to leave again."

"But she could get reborn."

"Yes, but she didn't know it then. Her name was Enya. You might have met her?"

"Can't say I have."

"She planted sunflowers on her way."

Homer's face lit up. "I did see a sunflower by the bridge one day, but it has long gone again, so I guess your friend found the way out eventually."

Nepomuk thought that this was likely the case and silently wished Enya a good life.

"Have you written anything new since, well, you arrived here?" asked Blanka.

"Me? Oh no. I have always been more of a story collector than a writer, to be honest," answered Homer.

"Something I always wondered, and the intellectuals still argue over, were you blind and had someone transcribe *The Iliad* and *Odyssey* for you?" asked Nepomuk.

Homer looked through him for a while. "Something like that. Anyway, do you think you know where you would like to settle down? Not that I don't like your company."

"Oh, no, we don't know, do we?" said Nepomuk to Blanka.

"I think maybe we need to go on a walk and have a look around by ourselves," said Blanka.

"And what better time to start than the morning, when everything is still fresh," said Homer and was almost too enthusiastic showing them out.

They wandered around for a while and found some more dwellings of people that were open for visitors. At one point, they stood on top of a hill and looked across the land when right under their feet a round door opened and someone barefoot and dressed in a cardigan and brown trousers stepped out and stretched.

"Oh, we're sorry," stammered Blanka.

The man jumped and screamed at them for standing on his roof, yammering that he hated visitors who intruded upon him in such a manner, and how one day he would just imagine an end to it by making the grass barbed wire.

Needless to say, Nepomuk and Blanka were not keen to become visitors to this abode and looked to put some distance between this underground house and their potential settlement.

They visited the Christmas village again, which was still cheerful, snowy, and on the brink of night, then the nudist beach, and a treehouse restaurant trail where the guests zi-plined from one restaurant to another, each with their own spectacular menus and views.

In the end though everything was just a short walk away from everything else and they decided to also settle near the stream. Nervous that they might put their cottage right next to an invisible neighbour or maybe even on top of them, they walked along the water until they found a nice spot with a nat-ural path between the trees that led to a meadow similar to the one that they had made by the River Styx.

To make sure that this place was unoccupied, they sat down for a picnic and listened to every noise and movement around them. Nothing unusual happened, apart from a Ger-man Shepherd, a zebra, and a very old Polar bear appearing briefly in the shrubs before reincarnating.

After a few hours they decided that this was it: this would become their forever after home, and they began mapping out where the rooms of their house would go. They began by put-ting their favourite furniture down first before building the cot-tage around it, to make sure that the rooms were spacious enough.

Once the walls, floors, windows, doors, and roof were there everything went easily. Nepomuk made some beautiful car-pets, whilst Blanka imagined paintings and family photos. They fixed shutters to the windows and flowerpots underneath filled with geraniums. Since they didn't need a kitchen here, they filled one room entirely with cushions and blankets and installed built-in bookshelves crammed with their favourite books, amongst them an original *Treasure Island*.

Then they moved on to the outside and planted an orchard from Nordic to tropical varieties, including a coconut palm as they had seen in Homer's house, just because they could. Daffodils around the tree trunks completed their romantic vision.

"I wished we could have some chickens," said Blanka when they finished several raised vegetable patches.

They didn't need to grow their own food, but it looked nice and gave them something to do.

"Yes, I guess we can't have everything, even in Paradise."

"Maybe we can get Cleo to live with us."

"Do you want to milk an Egyptian queen?"

"You're right, that'd be awkward."

They stood in the mouth of the little path to the river and looked at their creation and thought it looked good.

"We should invite Homer for tea," said Blanka.

"Yes. I also need to fetch my violin," said Nepomuk.

Hand in hand, they wandered over to their neighbour.

"I didn't think I'd see you again after all these months," said Homer, when they walked back after what had felt like an afternoon of work.

They apologized profusely and invited him for tea the next day, which he accepted gladly.

Nepomuk prepared several cakes and pastries for tea, scrapping half of them again. Somehow, he had trouble making up his mind and didn't have his usual feeling of pride, even after he had made a three-tiered cake fit for Marie Antoinette.

He finally settled on some simple scones with clotted cream and jam and Homer turned up just at the right time. Blanka had set the table under a tree that hung full of ripe cherries and Homer brought a self-made coconut sculpture as a housewarming gift. Blanka looked a little taken aback when she opened the card that came with it, which contained three stick figures with their names written in childlike handwriting.

After that day, they kept in touch and visited each other whenever convenient, which always seemed suitable when either of them turned up for a visit.

In between, Nepomuk and Blanka enjoyed themselves and tried everything that Paradise and its inhabitants had to offer. They found that playing volleyball naked was not their thing, but swimming naked in hot springs under the solitude of the moonlight was.

Surprisingly, Blanka was quite into white water rafting, while Nepomuk enjoyed free climbing the highest rocks he could find. Looking down from several kilometres, Paradise reminded him strongly of the shape of Neverland, and he wondered whether J.M. Barrie had known more than any living person.

They also made more friends besides Homer and rotated through visits on a daily basis. They got more and more comfortable with their ages and some days they were building sandcastles together as six-year-olds, only to have cocktails at the Tipi bar of the nudist beach at sunset. They went to restaurants and hip-hop clubs (something they had never done in their lifetime), went on sailing trips and snorkelled around colourful reefs that were quite disappointing as the fish, turtles, sharks, and even giant blue whales just turned up out of nowhere and disappeared before they could get a good look at them.

Everything seemed to be perfect and yet after a while – a long while, admittedly – all these fun adventures slowly became commonplace, almost trivial, and they found themselves staying at home more and more.

And then one morning, someone visited that Nepomuk had never expected. Knight Lukas turned up with a basket full of pineapples.

"How do you do, neighbour?" he asked.

"Very well, thank you," said Nepomuk, who had been walking around their garden, trying to find something to do.

"I come bearing gifts," Knight Lukas said, raising the basket. "It is so rare that you see your neighbours and I thought it would be nice for us to get to know each other."

Nepomuk was slightly confused. It appeared as if Knight Lukas did not remember him at all and then he remembered that he had looked fifty years older when they last met.

"Come in," he said politely. "You own the castle, right?"

"Manor, but yes. Childhood dream of mine."

"The best dreams."

Nepomuk led him around the house and to the cherry tree that never ran out of cherries.

"Can I offer you something to drink?" asked Nepomuk.

"How about some champagne to toast our friendship?"

"We usually don't start our morning with alcohol, but I can get you a glass and make ourselves some coffee."

"Of course, sure. Coffee is good, too," smiled Knight Lukas unshaken.

Nepomuk went inside and quickly prepared Blanka for their guest outside.

"Here we go. I didn't know how you take your coffee, so I brought out a range of things," said Nepomuk, carrying a fully laden tray in one hand and a tiered pastry stand in the other. "And this is my wife, Blanka."

"A pleasure to meet you," Knight Lukas said and got up to kiss her hand. "I wasn't sure when you talked about 'us', whether that was just your 'thing'. Some people around here are a little cuckoo, don't you think?"

"We have found everyone to be rather lovely," said Nepomuk.

"You live in that castle, right?" asked Blanka.

"Manor house, yes."

"Do you still have that cow?"

"Won't let me alone, day or night."

"Last time we saw you, you didn't seem too keen on her."

"You saw me? Oh, maybe. We all have our good and bad times, but I think we've come to a good agreement. And it's nice to have a companion, don't you agree?"

Chapter 22

KNIGHT LUKAS STAYED FOR a very, very long time, and as with everything here, time began to stretch uncomfortably the less enjoyably you spent it.

Knight Lukas told them all about his manor and the inspirations behind it, which was usually some very rich person back in his life, or the fact that he grew up poor, which almost made up for his overbearing need to talk. But then he also mentioned that he went to Harvard Business School and that his father had used contacts to get him his first job as a stockbroker, and they were not so sure anymore how many of the stories were true.

"Anyway, I'm so glad I found some pleasant folks to hang out with. Next time you're free, come to my humble residence and we'll have a party."

"We'll let you know," said Nepomuk.

"Just come by. Any time," Knight Lukas laughed.

After he had finally left, Nepomuk and Blanka sat in silence for a while, digesting their experience.

"I'm not sure I like him," Blanka finally said.

"I don't, but then I might be biased as I heard about a few of the things he did when he was alive," said Nepomuk.

"But he must have changed somehow, otherwise he wouldn't be here."

"I'm sure he has; he is much less obnoxious and seems to have at least some self-awareness now. Still, I'm not sure that this is enough to forgive what he has done."

The decision to see Knight Lukas again or not was taken out of their hands when he turned up again the next day, and the day after that, and every other day. They even tried to avoid him by going out around the times that he usually turned up, but he still managed to arrive exactly when they had come back and thought that they would have a little rest.

"I've decided to downsize," Knight Lukas told them one time. "You really should come round, you'll like it. It's a little cottage now."

"That is quite a change," said Nepomuk.

"Yeah, well. The other place was really too big. Could have played hide and seek with myself. Now, I only have what I need."

"How about we come for tea tomorrow?" suggested Blanka.

"Really? That would be great. I kept the bar for occasions like this."

Blanka later explained that she had felt sorry for Knight Lukas and maybe they should just get it over with and visit him.

Reluctantly, Nepomuk agreed to come with her the next day, and they were surprised to find an almost exact replica of their own cottage, except for the cushioned library where Knight Lukas had a billiard room with a bar.

"This is indeed very lovely," complimented Blanka. "Oh, is this your family?"

She had discovered some family photos on the wall.

"Ah, no. It's what I'm hoping for. Once I find a girlfriend, I will replace these photos."

"Oh."

"Yes. It does get pretty lonely when you have everything."

"It might be because everyone has everything," suggested Nepomuk.

"You're absolutely right. There is no way to distinguish yourself anymore; you can't get ahead of anyone," said Knight Lukas as if he had found a like-minded soul.

"Yes, here you have to be happy with yourself, and of course it helps if you were a good person to begin with."

"So true. It's still mind-boggling to me that they let everyone in here," Knight Lukas continued without getting Nepomuk's dig.

"Well, if you find that you are not happy with yourself, you can always move on and get a chance at a new life."

Knight Lukas ruminated on this briefly and Nepomuk hoped that he had taken the hint.

"It would surely help to make this place more attractive. I find that there are too many people who won't listen even if it is for their own good. That Homer guy, for instance, why is he so old? I suggested that he'd remember how he was when he was younger, but he just didn't care that he was an eyesore."

They sat through a very awkward afternoon and because Nepomuk had lost interest in talking to Knight Lukas, it was up to Blanka to carry the conversation.

"Good grief, what a terrible person," Blanka said when they were finally home again.

"I told you."

"He really needs to go back and get a different personality. No wonder no one wants to hang out with him if they don't have to."

"I think that's what he is struggling to understand. He has no hold over anyone here."

"It's almost as if Paradise could be your personal Hell if you are not cut out for it."

Nepomuk whole-heartedly agreed.

But it wasn't just Knight Lukas who seemed to struggle with this afterlife and the endless possibilities that it offered. Nepomuk also started to feel that all the food, excursions, experiences, and mundane items that were available at the whim of a thought started to feel hollow. How many times could they go on a sailing trip? Even if they imagined a storm and got swept away to a remote island, there was never a worry on their minds, as they could return home without even a scratch whenever they wanted.

Nepomuk created a little workroom for himself and began to learn how to make furniture from scratch, even going out to cut down a suitable tree. Blanka meanwhile learned pottery, wool spinning, archery, and built a 1958 Volkswagen Beetle.

They still visited friends but found that sooner or later people would disappear without a trace and all they could assume was that they had decided to be reborn. In their place, other people arrived, and they made new friends, but it got quite exhausting telling their story over and over again and be told how lucky they were for having stuck together even after death.

Nepomuk had just finished a garden set with beautiful mosaic inlays to replace their imagined set when he saw Blanka concentrating on shooting an arrow over seventy metres. She hit the bull's eye, relaxed, and concentrated again on her next shot. The arrows hit the gold every time, yet Blanka did not seem satisfied and eventually put the bow aside and just sat in the middle of their lawn.

"What's the matter?" Nepomuk asked her.

"I'm running out of things I want to do," said Blanka. "If I were alive, I would have won Olympic gold and broken several world records. But here, there is no point to any of it."

"Just as Homer said, you need to be happy with yourself."

Blanka nodded, defeated.

Nepomuk had just sat beside her when Knight Lukas turned up again.

"Howdy, fellas," he said and marched towards them in a complete cowboy outfit.

"Why are you wearing that?" asked Nepomuk.

"Oh, I thought I'd reinvent myself again."

"But there aren't any horses here and you only have one cow," said Blanka.

"It's the spirit that counts," said Knight Lukas.

"Are you trying to impress a girl?" Blanka asked outright.

"Maybe," Knight Lukas answered.

"You know, just be yourself and not some copy of someone that you think people will like."

Blanka was clearly not in the mood to play nice.

"But ... I don't think the person who I am, deep down, is likeable."

Nepomuk felt sorry for Knight Lukas for the first time.

"Sometimes, insight is the first step towards betterment," said Nepomuk.

"Are you agreeing with me?" asked Knight Lukas, upset.

"That you are an unlikeable arsehole? Yes."

Nepomuk instantly regretted having been that honest, but he was also tired of playing to the tune of someone he didn't like.

Knight Lukas turned on his heels and marched, spurs jingling, to the garden gate, where he stopped and stood kneading the fence post.

Nepomuk and Blanka watched, not sure what to do. They didn't want him to come back, but also knew they had been cruel.

Then, Knight Lukas did what they didn't want him to do. He came back.

"You are the only friends I have here, or at least I thought you were my friends. I don't have anybody, and I don't know how to change that. I can't change myself. God knows I've tried. This is who I am. I'm a narcissistic, materialistic arsehole who likes others to serve and worship him. I hate that no one here cares about the house or the cars I have, that no one depends on me and that no one wants to even attempt loving me. You two don't know how good you have it. Someone who is always by your side, makes you breakfast in bed, laughs at your jokes. Why can't I have something like that?"

"First of all, I don't laugh at all of Nepomuk's jokes, and if anything, we take turns making breakfast," said Blanka sternly.

"Minor difference," sulked Knight Lukas.

"It appears that your insight got lost somewhere in the last half of your speech. Wherever that first half came from, go there and start again."

"Do you know how exhausting that is? Seeing yourself for who you truly are? How embarrassing and painful?"

"No, I honestly don't."

"Well, maybe you don't have enough insight yet," snapped Knight Lukas.

Nepomuk and Blanka wished he would finally leave, preferably with the realization that he wasn't welcome here anymore.

"If you don't think you can change who you are now, maybe you should go and get reborn," suggested Blanka, and Nepomuk thought that was an excellent idea.

"What, and start from scratch, learn to walk and talk?"

"Start from scratch and hopefully become a better person," said Blanka persuasively.

"And how would I do that?"

"I don't know; I guess you just wish for it, imagine it?"

"You don't know how often I imagined being a billionaire with a hot wife, but nothing happened."

"I can imagine," mumbled Nepomuk.

"I don't think you can be that specific. After all, it is life that shapes you," said Blanka.

"Can I at least have rich parents?"

"I don't know. Maybe go and ask Homer about it."

"That old git? He's never been reborn himself. Probably too afraid cause he knows. He knows something."

"Maybe you are right. Maybe it's only the truly brave heroes who dare to take on life. Not like us scaredy cats who hide in Paradise," said Nepomuk.

"Maybe," said Knight Lukas. "Well, I won't bother you any longer. See you tomorrow, or not, sissies!" He laughed at them as he finally walked down the garden path and disappeared.

They were still sitting on the grass when Homer turned up.

"Hey, how are you two star-crossed lovers? Enjoying your day together?" he asked over the picket fence.

"Just starting to. Had a visitor who almost managed to spoil a day in Paradise," Nepomuk answered.

"Was it that Knight? I just saw him wandering around mumbling something about trumpets, muskets, and gates. I really don't think he'll make it much longer here," said Homer as he walked to them. "I hope I'm more welcome?"

"Much more," said Nepomuk.

"What a beautiful table," said Homer as they sat at Nepomuk's newly finished table.

"Thank you, I made it myself."

"Very talented."

"Can I ask you something," interrupted Blanka. "Assuming you wanted to reincarnate, how would you do that?"

"It's like you found this place. You need to be ready for it, no doubts in your heart and no fears in your head."

"And can you choose where you get reborn?"

"No, you only get to choose the type of being."

"So, you could be born into a troubled family?"

"Yes."

"Anywhere in the world."

"Yes."

"I guess you were right; it does take a brave hero to make that leap," said Blanka to Nepomuk.

"Are you two thinking of getting reborn?" asked Homer.

"No, of course not," said Blanka with an overly dramatic face. "But can I ask you a second question?"

"Sure," said Homer.

"Why have you never decided to get reborn?"

Homer paused for a moment. "Because I'm a coward."

They laughed, though Nepomuk thought that reincarnation might be closer to their minds and hearts than any of them admitted.

They had a lovely afternoon after all, gorging on comfort food and even a glass of mead that Homer had traded at the Christmas market.

Before they knew it, night was falling, and Homer retired to his own home.

That night, though, neither of them could sleep and Nepomuk listened to the crickets outside, the breeze in their curtains, and Blanka's regular breathing.

"Are you happy?" she suddenly asked.

"I am always happy, as long as we are together," he answered and wrapped himself around her. His answer was true, but in his heart, he had begun to wish to be alive again; with her, of course.

The next day, Knight Lukas did not come back.

Nepomuk began learning how to make stained glass windows and Blanka pushed the archery target back to a hundred metres.

Her first arrow hit the gold and she let her bow sink.

"What's up?" asked Nepomuk when she didn't pick up a new arrow.

"Are you truly happy here?" she asked him.

Nepomuk put his glass cutter down to look at her. "I am happy wherever you are. Are you happy?"

"I thought I was." Nepomuk walked over to her. "Why wouldn't anyone be happy in Paradise?" She had tears in her eyes. "It all just feels so pointless." Nepomuk hugged her.

"I think I know how you feel."

"Really?"

"Yes. Without any restraints, any struggle, without a finite lifetime, even the most enjoyable things start to feel empty."

They stood for a while holding each other.

"What are we going to do?" asked Blanka.

"I don't know," said Nepomuk, which was not true at all. "You could learn an instrument and we start a band?"

Blanka laughed. "You know what I meant."

"Or join a square dance group? I'm open to pretty much anything."

"Seriously."

"I have been thinking about reincarnation as well. It's just the coward in me that's afraid of losing you again."

"You waited twenty-two years for me in a desert where I could have arrived anywhere along the shore of an infinite river. I think you can find me in less time in a finite world of eight billion people."

Now, Nepomuk laughed. "I'm not sure I deserve this trust. I won't even remember you if we do this."

"That's a shame, 'cause I would remember you deep down in my heart as the love of my life."

Tears welled up and Nepomuk's heart was jumping in his throat. "I am so afraid of losing you though."

"I am much more afraid that if we stay here, we will lose the love we have and will be even worse off. And just in case we don't find each other on Earth, we could tell Homer to remind us when we are dead again."

"Like a contingency plan."

"Like Cupid in an old man's body. Come on, let's talk to him."

Blanka led him gently down their garden path and out the gate.

Homer was surprised to see them that early in the day but welcomed them in. He was just making another coconut figure that looked only slightly less deformed than his other creations.

They explained to him what they had talked about and he didn't seem surprised at all.

"It takes a lot of strength to take the leap, but even more to stay."

"Do you think you will recognize us when we come back?" asked Blanka nervously.

"Just like the last times you were here," he said with a smile.

"We've done this before?" asked Nepomuk.

"Every single time. But I won't give up hope that one day you'll stay and keep me company."

"Why don't you come with us?" asked Blanka.

"I told you, because I'm a coward. Besides, if something does go wrong down there, who would tell you two love birds to find each other when you come back?"

With lots of tears but light hearts they said goodbye to the old man. Before they left, Homer pulled Nepomuk aside.

"I've never told this to anyone, but I truly only stay because I am such a coward."

"I don't think you're a coward for staying here."

"Oh, but I am. You see, I've never done anything impressive in my life. I was useless at everything, still am; just look at my sculptures."

"But you've written two of the world's greatest books."

"I haven't. For whatever reason, people just began ascribing them to me and I was never honest enough to tell the truth. You see, if you've never done anything and everyone laughed at you when you failed at the simplest things, having people admire you is magical."

"But taking credit for someone else's work is fraudulent."

"I know, I know. But I have nothing else and I'm afraid I will never amount to anything, even if I gave life another shot. So, there you go. That is my secret, my cowardly reason for staying here."

"Why are you telling me this now?"

"Because you won't remember when you're reborn. I just needed to let it out to a friend."

Nepomuk nodded silently. Somehow, he was sad that a great person like Homer had turned out to be the greatest coward of them all.

"I guess I'll see you when we come back."

"I'll be here."

They hugged a last time and Nepomuk joined Blanka, who was waiting by the river.

"What did you two have to talk about?" she asked curiously.

Nepomuk didn't see why he couldn't tell Blanka, since she would forget Homer's secret as well and it felt good to share upsetting things.

"Are you afraid?" Nepomuk asked her when they stood facing each other under their cherry tree.

"No. If anything, I'm excited. I wonder who I will be and how my life will turn out," Blanka said.

"It is quite exhilarating," admitted Nepomuk. "And knowing that we have done this before makes me less nervous."

"Are you ready?"

"I think so, yes."

They squeezed each other's hands.

"Wait," said Nepomuk. "I need to remember to bring some seeds with me next time."

"Grass would be nice," smiled Blanka.

"And maybe some cherries," said Nepomuk.

"Come and find me."

Nepomuk felt Blanka's warm hands in his for a long time, but her voice echoed in his head even longer, even after their cottage garden and the canopy of the cherry tree had long dissolved.

He was surrounded by warmth, feeling secure even though he didn't know where he was nor who he was. All he knew was that everything would be alright.

A Short Thank You

I would like to thank my editor Nick for her great work in jigging my words into coherent sentences.

This book would not have come to be without three words that were given to me by my most patient and supportive husband, critique, and cheerleader Yan.

ℬAKER - 𝒞OIN - 𝒫LAIN

If you liked Amantos, please remember to leave a review or a simple star-rating.

Thank you very much for reading!

Herman Recipes

BASE DOUGH

- 100g wheat flour
- 1 tablespoon sugar
- 2 teaspoons of dry yeast
- 150ml lukewarm water

Mix ingredients in a bowl or jar made from glass or plastic (not metal, as this interferes with the liveliness of the yeast). Use a wood or plastic spoon to mix everything to a liquid dough.

Keep the dough in a container with a closed lid at room temperature for the first 2 days and stir once a day. Make sure the lid is only loosely placed to allow any developing gas to escape.

After 2 days, the dough should show small bubbles on the surface due to the ongoing lactic acid fermentation that should have started.

Continue as follows:

Day 1: rest
Day 2: stir
Day 3: stir
Day 4: stir
Day 5: feed – 100g wheat flour, 150g sugar, 150ml milk; stir well
Day 6: stir
Day 7: stir

Day 8: stir
Day 9: stir
Day 10: feed – 100g wheat flour, 150g sugar, 150ml milk;
stir well

After the second feed, Herman is ready to be used. Make sure to keep 200g of the dough and start again at day 1.

You can give 200g to a friend to start their own Herman, therefore Herman is also called the Friendship Bread.

TIP 1: You can freeze portions of Herman just in case you go on a holiday or cannot look after him for a while.

TIP 2: The recipe is quite sweet and best suited for cakes or sweet rolls. You can use only 2 tablespoons instead of 150g sugar when feeding Herman to create a more savoury dough.

TIP 3: Keeping Herman in the fridge from day 1 slows down the fermentation process and makes for a milder flavour. Keeping Herman at room temperature will result in a more malty flavour, great for more savoury breads.

TIP 4: Herman's brother Siegfried is made with rye flour and less sugar perfectly suited for savoury bread. Experiment with different flour types or mix them to find your own perfect dough.

WHAT TO DO WITH HERMAN?

<u>Juicy Herman Cake</u>

- 200g of Herman
- 200g wheat flour
- 100g sugar
- 200ml milk
- 100ml oil
- 3 eggs
- 1 teaspoon of vanilla sugar
- pinch of salt
- 2 tablespoon of baking soda

Optional:
- 100g of chopped or sliced nuts, almonds, raisins, chocolate, ...

Mix all ingredients to a smooth dough

Fill into an oiled cake tin (loaf or bun)

Bake at 180°C (160°C convection oven) for 45-55 minutes

Simple Herman Bread

- 200g Herman
- 250g wheat flour
- 250g full grain wheat or rye flour
- 300ml water
- ½ tablespoon salt
- 1 pack of dry yeast or ½ a cube of fresh yeast

Dissolve the yeast in the lukewarm water

Knead all ingredients to a smooth and elastic dough that does not stick to the bowl (add flour or water as necessary)

Let the dough rest at room temperature for 2h to rise

Knead the dough and either form a loaf on a baking tray or fill into an oiled and floured loaf tin.

Let the dough rest again at room temperature for 45-60 minutes

Bake at 190°C (170°C convection oven) for 40-45 minutes

Sweet Sunday Rolls

- 400g Herman
- 500g wheat flour
- 80g soft butter
- 1 egg
- 1 teaspoon of salt
- 15g of yeast
- 100ml milk

Dissolve the yeast in the lukewarm milk

Mix all ingredients to a smooth and elastic dough that does not stick to the bowl (add flour or milk as necessary)

Let the dough rest at room temperature for 1h to rise

Knead the dough and form 8-10 equal size balls (you can also braid the dough).

Let the raw rolls rest again at room temperature on the baking tray for 30 minutes

Bake at 200°C (170°C convection oven) for 25 minutes